An Inflammable Act of Kindness

An Inflammable Act of Kindness

Monika Killeen

992 Press

Published by 99% Press,

an imprint of Lasavia Publishing Ltd.

Auckland, New Zealand

www.lasaviapublishing.com

ISBN: 978-1-991083-14-2

In memory of my grandmother,
Wilma Barbierikova 1934-2019
With love and gratitude forever

Contents

Chapter 1

White Deer

2020

London, outside of the M25

'Muum? Where is she, do you know?' Eliza shouts across the house, exasperated, to her headphones-wearing brother. 'Mum? Burt! Where is she? Muum?' She stampedes into Burt's room like a herd of wild horses and lifting the headphone off his ear with the threat of it boomeranging, she exhales the words, 'where-is-she?'

'No idea. She probably left. For good.' Burt doesn't lift his eyes off his device, his fingers still moving rapidly. To kill or to run for his life.

'So not funny. Mum!' Letting the headphone go with a bang, taking no notice of Burt's threats of deadly revenge. She heard them all before. 'Muuum? Ah! Here you are! Why are you ignoring me?' All three an accusation.

Meli feels like saying stop calling me names. 'Sorry, Eli, I didn't hear you. I was just thinking about something.' This is a lie. Meli did hear Eliza. She was just hiding, a small act of passive aggression that earned her an extra moment to herself. Her children never stopped expecting her to just materialise. They called, she appeared. That was the equation.

'Can you not do two things at the same time? Most people can think and hear at the same time?' Eliza is still outraged.

'Good question,' she says to Eliza as she decides on diversion. She is not in the mood to enter into a battle with a smaller version of herself. This other version has way more energy, and, sometimes, way more clarity to her argument. Seeing a moment of hesitation in Eliza's eyes, she continues, 'Freud said the best way to listen to someone is with what he called an evenly suspended attention. This means you are listening while thinking and not thinking at the same time. Interesting, right?'

'Err, ok. I have no idea what that means. How can you think and not think at the same time?' Eliza says.

Meli smiles. 'It is just doing two things at the same time, Eli.' It is a small win but a win nonetheless. It is also a paradox, which life is basically made up of, but that is an onion layer to be left to be unpeeled for another day. 'It is like you only think about what someone is saying but not about what you want to say back. So you suspend your thoughts about what you think you know and want to say, and you just listen and think about what the other person is saying. Nothing else.'

'That's thinking.' Eliza won't be defeated easily.

'It is thinking about something and not thinking about something. So it is thinking and not thinking at the same time. Anyway. You wanted me?'

'Yes. Can I make pancakes?'

Eliza is eight. A couple of years ago, she told someone that her mother was a psychic-therapist, but that really Meli was psychic like a wizard or a witch, depends on the time of the day, and Eliza was the therapist. Together they were a psychic-therapist. And one day, Eliza would be both because she wanted to be like Mum, the queen of the castle, coup d'état on the way already, without knowing it. Eliza liked playing with words. She also liked playing to an audience. At the time, they were having Eliza's nails done, her birthday treat, and she wasn't sure of the effect of what she was saying and was scrutinising her mother's face as she was saying it. Only seeing love back, she went right on.

'Sure. Can you try not to burn yourself again? People will think...'

'Mum. That was years ago.'

'Three weeks.'

'Same thing, basically.' Eliza says as she skips off.

Eliza still can't just walk. She skipped before she would walk. It was one of the sunny things about her. There were many. Then she comes to a halt. You can almost hear the screeching of the brakes, stopping her body, Tom to her inner Jerry, because she just thought of something. Something that absolutely can't wait.

'Oh and mum?'

'Yes, Eli?'

'That Fraud guy, he probably wasn't a very good parent. I think it is quite rude to not listen properly when someone is talking to you.' And with that she was gone.

Meli mutters to the room. 'You weren't listening, Eliza. It wasn't listening and not listening, it was thinking and not thinking.'

She walks off to her computer to find the concept's definition. Was there a website, "Freud for kids"?

Listening to the upbeat sounds of Eliza cluttering about in the kitchen, and Burt, hurling abuse at his co-players on some video-game-on-mute, Meli sits down and takes a sip of her coffee. She is in her office. For this precise moment, all is as it should be. She loves these tiny moments. Looking out of the window, she spots a large white deer. He comes every now and then, patrolling the fields that spread around the back of her house, a boundary formed by a deep line of trees. The trees are beautiful this time of the year. They look like a Monet painting. She cannot understand how she didn't notice these things before. Like the sunset. She thinks of the white deer, looking at it looking at her. As a young girl, she would have ascribed a meaning to these appearances of the mystical deer. An omen of good luck or bad. Mother won't be home too late tonight. Father will not wake up if she is late. Seeing the deer would mean one or the other. It helped her, this world of her own in her head, where she could control things by magical thinking to help her cope with the world made for her by others outside her head.

Meli is about to see a client. She is putting herself in the listening and thinking mode. It is a bit like picking up from the floor of her mind all the thoughts and feelings she ever had and putting them away in an airing cupboard, out of sight, out of mind. She will be temporarily disabling all access to this storage facility. Her mind emptied out, now a nice, clean chest of drawers, ready to receive other people's unprocessed laundry, which needed to be sorted, unfolded, aired, folded back, some thrown out and some long-forgotten ones remembered. It never changes. The tremor of nervous energy. Every fifty minutes with a client is like two children meeting together for the first time in her room. Will they get on? Will they like each other? It's always like this, no matter how many times she has done this walk into her office, taken a seat in her ocean-blue armchair, while waiting for a client to take the seat opposite, but not directly opposite. That feels too confrontational, too much in her face, too much of her face in their face. Side on allows for more perspectives, a bit like when people sit in the car next to each other. It can make it easier to talk, away from the glare of the other's eye.

She wonders what it means for the forthcoming session that she is taken back to her childhood by the mystical white deer. Some clients she looks forward to seeing. Some, it takes some effort to really see through the words they have to say. They are all fascinating.

'Why do you say that?'

'That it is sad?'

'Yes.'

'You don't think it is sad.'

'No. Well, at least I never did before now. But I can sort of see what you mean. I never thought of it like that before.'

'No.'

Meryl is crying her silent tears, dabbing her eye make-up, trying to force the tears back in where they came from.

It is hard for Meryl to accept that her mother was anything but kind and loving. Meryl was seventy-six years old when she came to see Meli. That was two years ago. Her fourth marriage was falling apart. She didn't want to go through it again. Meryl had two daughters, two granddaughters and one great-granddaughter. Neither the daughters nor the granddaughter were in a stable relationship. Meryl never thought it was sad that she left her family home when she was sixteen, pregnant and alone. She also didn't think it was sad when her family, including her six siblings, moved to Australia when she was twenty-one. With the eldest and closest sibling already in the

States, not speaking to their father, and one in Ireland, not speaking to anyone, she was alone with two small children and an abusive partner. Still she did not see it was sad.

'I think I just thought it was pretty exciting.' Meryl says after a while. 'I didn't think it was dangerous. I didn't realise how hard it would be. My mum was ok with me leaving, so I guess I thought it must be ok.'

'Hm.' Meli nods.

'I mean, if she didn't think it was ok, she wouldn't have let me go. Would she?' was that a doubt, Meli wonders. Is it beginning to be allowed in?

'She was a very kind woman. She would not have let me go if she didn't think it would be ok.' Saying this more to herself than Meli, Meryl is looking down at her feet, thoughtful.

'It really feels that she wouldn't have let you go if she didn't think it would be ok.' Meli pauses before adding, 'But things weren't all that ok. You were sixteen, pregnant and alone, in a bedsit with a woman whose son was in prison.'

'Yes. That doesn't sound that ok to me now,' Meryl says, uncomfortably shifting in her chair. It is hard for her. It was so long ago. Her mum dead. Who wanted to speak ill of the dead?

'No. It doesn't.' Meli says, gently as she can, wishing once again she could at this point deliver a small lecture about psychotherapy. It would sound something like this. "This is not an attack on your mum. This is to try and understand things better. To free you to feel your feelings without worrying about what others might think. No judgment." Judgment was the thing that prevailed in all Meryl's relationships. No one came up to anyone's harsh standards. Everyone survived by putting everyone else down and therefore no one stayed with anyone. Tied in an uninterrupted generational cycle of misery, splitting the world into good and bad, idealising one, demonising another. Meryl idealised her mother beyond any realm of normal. So now it would be hard to start trying to see her as she really was. Not a demon. Not the angel either.

Meli wishes she could explain this all to Meryl, but she can't. Meli's therapy is not directive or didactic. You don't give advice. You don't explain. You listen. And you ask questions. And you reflect like a good mirror so that they can see themselves properly, sometimes for the first time. It is no mean feat to mirror the judgement within, without making the person feel judged in the moment, and without explaining. Meli forces her attention back to Meryl who is now speaking-in-defence again,

'...She was busy with the other three and father was going through something then. She was busy. She looked after all of us. She loved us.'

Meli stays silent. How do you say, she did but not in the right way. She did, but her understanding of love was based on a wrong template. You don't. You wait.

'There is this memory I have about a family wedding,' Meryl says after a moment of silence. 'It was years later. They came back for it from Australia. I saw her holding Eddie's hand. He was in his twenties then. She never held my hand. I remember thinking, that's strange.'

'You remember *thinking* it was strange?'

'Yes, I remember thinking it felt strange to realise she never held my hand.'

'You remember *thinking* it *felt* strange.' The emphasis on those two words was hard to discern for Meryl. Meli wondered if it was too soon to make it. Some people are scared of bridging their thoughts with their feelings. There is just a faint white noise of dissonance. The filtering mind says to its subordinate, the feelings, instead of sad you'll be angry, and the feelings go, oh ok that's easy. They harden with it over the years.

Meli thinks, that barrier between thinking and feeling is like an invisible brick wall. Only occasionally will Meryl let herself come out of her shell, like a snail, slowly, carefully, checking out the outside with the feelers at the top of its head, quickly retreating to the safety of its shell at the first sign of anything because anything signals possible danger. Living safe, living in the dark. Is that living? Perceiving everything outside as danger. What kind of a life is that?

'I suppose thinking something is not the same as feeling something.' Meli ventures. 'I am wondering if by saying you were thinking something helps you to not feel something which might be overwhelming, somehow too much. Thinking it was strange that your mother was holding your younger brother's hand was preferable to recognising it hurt to see that because she never held your hand.'

There was a heavy pause.

'Yes, I felt like I was left out of something.'

'What were you left out of, Meryl?'

'I don't know. Like they were in a club in which I had no membership. I was just a visitor.'

Fifty minutes is up. Meryl would feel again and again like she was being left out of something. When Meli would end the session, it would feel to Meryl that Meli was going to go onto holding someone else's hand.

After the session, Meli stays in the room for a while. She lets it percolate, this awful sense of sunken abandonment, to feel it, to get some measure of it. She will have to mould it in her mind in different shapes and forms before she can give it back to Meryl to find it, this feeling that she could not bear to own, not yet. They often say, if I start crying, I worry I will never stop. But they do.

It weighed heavily on Meli. Mothers and daughters. The inevitable initial closeness, an actual, not metaphorical, cord tying them together for nine months. It doesn't get much closer than that. And then, snip, cord is no more, followed by the more or less gradual separation that will go on and on. The loss of the cord that ties you to another is a loss of something that was once a part of you. Even though you think you don't remember it, your body docs. It is where utopia is born. It is not a loss of an identity because you don't yet have one. Once you are snipped free, you go on to try to find one, followed as you go by the memory of once being at one with another, followed by blame, the guilt, the love, the hate, the sorrow, the sense of loss and a desire to find the impossible.

Making her way into the kitchen, Meli is snatched back into the reality of her kitchen without a warm-up. Her children are talking at her in stereo. This is a skill they excel at and one she would never master.

'Please stop. One of you, please stop talking. One at a time, remember?'

Nothing. Stereo made up of their voices on too loud. They can't hear her.

'Stop!' It comes out loud. Too loud.

'Mum. Why are you shouting?' She stands accused again.

Chapter 2

Bunny Little Ear

1980s-1990s

A small town in a little country in the shadow of the recent Russian invasion

Meli is lying down propped up by a heap of embroidered cushions on an old divan in her great-grandmother's kitchen. The room smells of fresh dough. She is leafing through a picture book about a small rabbit called Bunny Little Ear. In the story, Little Ear sets off to find himself a life in the big, far-away world. And to find out what he is made of, out there in the world. Will he have to fight dragons or evil spirits? Will he find himself a Princess? It is a world beyond the warmth of his mother's kitchen, a world which seems a lot of fun and full of promise of things to come, things he hasn't seen, things he didn't know but feels inexorably drawn to. Because as lovely as everything is in their kitchen and the woods he knows, Little Ear is bored. A world out there, like a magnet, pulling him in. There is no resisting magnetic forces. Meli starts to imagine her own future without knowing it. Bunny Little Ear always planned to come back with the spoils and return to his mother.

Meli is ill, and that's why she is at her *Nagymama's* home. *Nagymama* is her grandma's mum. She is a little old lady, with white hair all the way to her waist, pleated neatly and wearing the traditional folk clothes that mark a widow. Meli often stays in this tiny kitchen watching *nagymama* kneading the dough. Meli is often ill these days. *Nagymama* makes the best fresh egg noodles and will keep on making them to her last day. She only speaks Hungarian even though she lives in Czechoslovakia and always has. Meli doesn't yet speak Hungarian, even though the majority of the old people here can only speak it. This lingual quirk arose from the period of the Austro-Hungarian Empire, or the Dual Monarchy, which ruled the little country until the First World War, when it came under a new rule, and everyone was to learn Slovakian, and after the Second World War, Russian. But such thoughts would be a bit later for Meli. For now, there isn't much talking between her and her great grandmother. Meli would briefly wonder if this is normal, not that Austria and Hungary formed a military and diplomatic alliance, but if it was normal she was left in the care of someone with whom she could not speak common language. But Mother has to go to work and so does grandma. Meli is only three or so. Maybe talking to each other isn't that important. It feels fine anyway. *Nagymama* is nice. And tiny.

When Meli is ill she spends a lot of time hallucinating due to dangerously high temperatures that will burn her into madness. Maybe she is hallucinating herself out of that world, a world where anxiety runs so deep it threatens to drown her world at her home. Last night mother and father were not nice to each other again. But Meli is not sure what is real and what is not. She was burning at 41C most of the night.

She is feeling better now. Soon, her eyes heavy, she drifts off to a restful sleep with the sun peering through the crocheted curtains in *nagymama's* kitchen window, stroking her face gently with its warm hand.

'Meli, Meli, wake up, Meli, it's just a dream. It's not real.' The sound of her mother's voice finally breaks through the horrific sensation that she was lying in a snake pit. They were everywhere. They were heaving around, intertwined so that she could not tell the ending or beginning of them. They brushed against her burning skin with their coarse, scaly surface. Enmeshed in one ginormous hug, hissing their contentment in the gentle sway, she knew this cosiness was a trap. They were not there to comfort her. They were a threat.

'Meli, can you hear me?'

She blinks and rubs her eyes. She nods, confused. 'Mami, there are snakes here. In my bed.'

'No, Meli, Little Heart, look, you are in my bed and there are no snakes. We checked already but we can check again. Look, I will switch the big light on so you can see. No snakes. See? No snakes anywhere.'

Her mother is patient, pleading, wanting desperately for Meli to come out of this horrible dream. It scares her mother to see Meli like this. She feels guilty. It is probably her fault for not spotting something was wrong earlier. She should have taken her to see a doctor when she said she was not feeling well. But she prefers to go to work. It is fun at work and it is not so much fun looking after a child when you are twenty and have other things on your mind like the university you didn't get to go to because you fell pregnant on your first time. Life is not fair.

Meli sees. There are no snakes now. There is only a bed with a sheet crumpled under her little body trying to wriggle out of the dread that was her dream. She sees it but she doesn't believe it.

'Mami, I think they are hiding. They must be. They were definitely here.' Small voice, eyes wide with fear.

'No. Come. We will search the whole room. Let's get out of this bed for a minute. We will look under the bed and in the wardrobe and everywhere.' Her mother hopes this will wake Meli up from the nightmare that is still there even in her waking state.

After the search, Meli watches her mum straightening the sheets for her, smoothing out any bumps that could feel wrong. Meli loves her mum then so hard it hurts. She wakes up for her. She is patient with her, kind and warm. Why does she have to be sick for her mother to be nice?

When Meli finally falls asleep her mother doesn't hold her. Maybe Meli is just too hot, too hot to touch. But she is there. Her mother is there, right next to her, ready to wake up if Meli needs her. Maybe things will be ok yet.

When she comes to collect her from *nagymama's* the following afternoon, her mother wears a black eye, not hidden behind her green eyeshadow.

'Just pull them up for God's sake! How hard can it be?' Mother is shouting from the bathroom, while trying to get rid of the lingering presence of alcohol. It's on her breath, in her hair, on her skin, and on her mind. That's the worst bit. Her father already left for work. He leaves the house at 5am when it is still dark outside.

Actually, Meli thinks, it is fucking hard, to be honest. The 1980s tights for eight-year-olds are a nightmare to pull up with the stupid, meandering seams that snake around the leg in an incomprehensible twist which makes them feel like pressure tights, putting the pressure in all the wrong places.

Meli swears now, only in her head, but it feels good. It is like hitting something, only with a word instead of a fist.

Why does everything have to be so hard? She starts crying quietly. She doesn't want her mother to see because that will make her feel guilty which will make her shout even more. Too late.

'Oh for God's sake! What is it now? Come here!'

She pulls harshly on the tights, hurting Meli until the stupid things are finally on. They rush to the car, sliding gingerly on the icy pavement, only to find out the windscreen is frozen with freshly fallen snow. They will be late again. Meli watches her mother's bare fingers scraping the snow off the window going raw with the cold. Why wouldn't she put the gloves on? Why does she always put herself in a place of hurt? Is that a punishment? The car huffs and puffs before it reluctantly agrees to wake up.

They are late because mother was late to bed. Too much wine, too much shouting. Tears, chairs banging and hands slamming tables, loud, angry voices. The snow looks beautiful. It covers up all the mess. It makes everything seem perfect.

Chapter 3

Girls Don't Just Want To Have Fun

1980s-1990s

A small town in a little country

Meli is twelve. She has decided to go to boarding school this September. Boarding schools in Czechoslovakia, as her country will be known until 1992, operate from old nunneries and are run by women who are approximately as maternal as a childless nun might be imagined to be. In the bigger picture, that is the picture framing the smaller picture of Meli's immediate surroundings, these years see a lot of unsettledness in the country. Dissatisfaction with the rule of the Communist Party will eventually lead to the bloodless Velvet Revolution of 1989. Gone will be the Czechoslovak Socialist Republic. Enter the Czech Republic and Slovakia. Exit the Czech Socialist Republic and the Slovak Socialist Republic. It is just one word, Socialist, they take exception to. They lived with it for thirty years. Maybe that is how long it takes to grow up or into an opinion, an opinion that can form an idea, a new construct. Thus democracy begins.

In the smaller picture, which in many ways mirrors the tumultuous mood of Meli's country, the days of hallucinating herself out of a family drama are gone. What's left of it is a crab-shell legacy – as if those high temperatures crystalised her surface layer into something hard yet capable of shedding. She was either going to don the shell so that she could not feel anything, except perhaps some resonance should something touch her, or, she would bare all to expose the ugly nerve endings to shock the other into a retreat. This way, she would always be at a safe distance, never too close. One thing is for sure. She is never going to be like her mother. Crab-like, Meli also grew pincer claws, which she uses in unequal measure to feed herself, to defend and to woo her prey. Her mother's version of their species didn't grow these. They didn't have them back then, not in their neck of the woods, where all little red riding hoods were sticking to the path.

'Meli, Meli, here!' Comes a hushed cry, her best friend Gabi manically waving from behind a rubbish container in the corner of the dorm's courtyard. They are not supposed to smoke in the dorm, obviously. In fact, they are not supposed to smoke at all, and if they are found out, there will be trouble. Gabi managed to steal a couple of cigarettes from her dad. An older student eyes them suspiciously as she walks past putting her rubbish out, but says nothing. Meli and Gabi are quite famous within the roomy confines of the old nunnery repurposed to house the dreams of teenage girls, training them to become primary school teachers. To the outside world, they seem a bit of a good cop, bad cop sort of thing, or maybe a Thelma to her Louise, depending on the way you see things. Gabi is short and funny, with beautiful red hair cascading down her head in all its wavy directions. Meli is tall and outrageous. She breaks all the rules in the book and seems to get away with it, which can cause a lot of outrage. Meli doesn't have beautiful hair. Mousy brown. What a stupid expression, she thinks, but it is true.

'Hey, that little weasel is on your case, isn't she?' Gabi says as she passes Meli a lit cigarette.

The little weasel is their psychology tutor who indeed is on Meli's case. It is unclear to Meli why as she actually finds psychology interesting. Having said that, every time Meli sees her tutor, she is filled with a mixture of repulsion, fear and inexplicably, a reluctant desire for her tutor's approval. Meli is sure her face betrays her. She will never get the weasel's approval. In fact, despite her incredibly competent performance at the psychology A level oral exam, four years later, the weasel will only give her a B. Swings and roundabouts though, her PE tutor will give her an A, when really, she will not be an A in PE ever. Meli knows her PE tutor likes her a little bit, in a way that will not be approved of by her psychology tutor. A lot of men do. Meli thinks this is actually quite useful. If life gives you lemons, you have to try to make something of it, somehow.

'Yes, she is, the ugly dwarf thing. I don't get it.'

'No, me neither, you actually listen during her class. Seems unfair,' says Gabi, thoughtfully adding, 'fuck her, Mels, she is ugly and her life is probably shit. Let's face it, who would want to fuck her or love her, looking that way? She's probably just jealous.'

'Another dwarf?'

'Imagine that.' Says Gabi, pulling on her cigarette like her life depends on it.

'I'd rather not.'

'Seven little dwarves coming for some chitty chitty bang bang.' Gabi's on a roll now, and they laugh.

'Do you think he likes me?' Meli says, changing the subject.

'Who? Oh. Yes.'

'I might go with him tomorrow. He asked me over to his. His mum is out,' a sparkle in Meli's eye as she says this, 'what do you think?'

'Shiii-it. You serious? You are.' Gabi answering her own question is just as excited. She lives her life through Meli, the more exciting parts of it, anyway. Although she got Meli smoking.

'Just make sure you tell me all about it and for God's sake don't be late for the doors. I really don't fancy having to make up another sprained-my-ankle-story. Plus it might look suspicious if I was to fall down them stairs again. I mean who does that? Thunder only strikes once and all that. Even the matrons know that.'

'Is it thunder or lightning?' Meli asks.

'Well, I'd say you might yet see both if you are late for the doors again.'

The doors of the dorm are locked every day with a key kept in the matron's office at half past four in the winter and five in the summer.

'I think it's immoral to be honest,' says Meli as she inhales and tries to blow a perfect smoke ring.

'What,' Gabi says, alarmed, 'he is not sleeping with that girl from form four anymore is he?'

'No. The door is being locked like we're some kind of animals, herded in, or, worse still, nuns. I mean, what does it do to you long term, like having this kind of boundary imposed on your freedom? Do you know what I mean?' Meli is warming up.

'Stops you from getting pregnant, I guess,' says Gabi, pouring some cold over Meli's heat, and then, 'shit Melsie, imagine you as a nun,' and she bursts out laughing. 'Poor God, that's all I have to say.'

They laugh, but Meli is thinking, what did she do putting herself here? It was her idea after all, the dorm. It suddenly occurs to her that it was she who imposed this boundary on herself like someone might put a leash on a dog. She put a leash on her inner animal. She hopes she won't strangle on it. Out of one frying pan into another.

They put their cigarettes out and sneak up the back stairs trying to avoid a matron before they can brush their teeth and get a gum to mask the smell. But it is the smell of their futures, and it won't be hidden. It's coming, ready or not.

Upstairs in their room, Betty has a new love interest but she will only tell Tania. Tania is busy dying her dark thick hair blonde, applying undiluted peroxide while listening to Betty. It will end up orange for about two years, before it will finally look blonde, not thick anymore. Martina is on the top bunk preparing for the maths test they have the following day. Meli opens her wardrobe.

'Shit,' she mutters as a large heap of unfolded clothes falls out as if saying, fuck you, not living like this anymore. Fold us up and put us in neatly. Meli shares the wardrobe with Gabi. Her half, a row of soldiers.

'Hey, G, what shall I wear tomorrow?' They love this topic.

Eventually, the whole room joins in with a bit of a view on things. Too slutty. Too boring. Too red. Too long. Not you.

'What about that green one, it really brings your eyes out.' Someone says.

Her eyes. Meli thinks they are too little and her eyelashes too thin. Also, she is almost blind. When you can't see, you find other ways. Still a lot of people say things about her eyes. Some boys in town call her the Cat, something to do with her green eyes. Later she would dye her hair black, ready for her own *Tournee du Chat Noir*. She will be getting this show on the road soon. She can't wait. All that life out there to be found. Town to town. New acts. Each more daring than the last. For now though, Meli is a blonde. She also used undiluted peroxide to make it happen. It only takes a couple of goes. Her hair, like her, is open to change. Right now Meli is a blonde and her ideal woman is a mixture of Marlene, Marilyn and Madonna. Four Ms.

A month later they are by the bins again. In between the perfectly formed smoky clouds, Meli tells Gabi, 'I missed my periods.'

'Shiii-it.' Gabi says.

Chapter 4

Why Do You Always

1990s - 2000s

Central London

They had a row. Last night he was late home. It is always the same. He would stop answering her messages or calls. She understands. She wouldn't have wanted to hear from herself either. She behaves like an ugly little despot then, in those moments, summoning him home, belligerent, threatening, demanding he stop having fun, because what if he did something stupid? What then? Except Don doesn't do stupid things. But she can't believe it. It is a bit like those snakes. Are they less real when they are not real if it real-ly feels like they are there? No, they are not.

They sit on a couch absentmindedly watching news on a 24/7 cycle. She saw that budget announcement three times already, two wine glasses ago. It is still largely incomprehensibly boring to her. Possibly it is incomprehensible because it is so boring.

'Why do you always have to do that?' As soon as she says this, she knows that's not true. He doesn't *always* do that, but whatever *that* is, it feels like something that *always* happens to her. It *always* feels threatening.

'Do what?'

'You know what.'

'Nope. I went out. Had a few beers. Came home. No one died.'

'You ignored me. That's not nice or reasonable.'

'You weren't going to be nice if I didn't ignore you, or reasonable.'

'Because you lied.'

'I didn't.'

He is right. He didn't lie. She had asked him not to be late because she couldn't sleep, because she had work to do in the morning, because if she didn't sleep she would be fucked the next day and it was a big day at work. Like he was responsible for her state of mind. But she was not about to start being reasonable now. She was going to court the next day, and, it turned out, she hated public speaking. Her voice was a leaf in the wind. She just needed him to bend to her need on this occasion, because on these occasions, she didn't know how else to be.

She qualified as a lawyer a few years ago. It took her four years working as a legal executive trainee to do it, a different route than law school. Some, the wig wearers, looked down on it. Others embraced it while paying you less. Anyway, she was one of only seven in the whole of the UK to qualify as a legal executive advocate, which gave her rights of audience in criminal courts, which meant the night before any court appearance would not see Meli being reasonable. She would only be on high alert.

'You implied by not saying anything to the contrary that you would be considerate of my state of mind about my big day at court. You know I am new to this and it makes me really nervous and not having a good night's sleep can be the straw.'

'How did it go?'

'Not the point.'

'What is the point?'

'That you promised me something and you didn't do it. It feels like I don't matter, what I feel doesn't matter. You just bulldoze right through it if you decide it is not a big deal.'

'That's not true.'

'To me it is.'

Don gets up. He doesn't want to carry on with this conversation. It only ever has one end.

'Don't walk away. Why do you always walk away?'

'I don't want to talk about it when you're like this.' Don pulls the door behind him. He will be going upstairs putting his headphones on, shutting her out. The noise that she could become. Relentless. The noise that doesn't hear.

'When I'm like what?' Meli shouts after him. This is abuse. Is this abuse? No, it probably isn't. She knows that when Don is late like this it makes her relive something she has tried long and hard to distance herself from, something she did distance herself from. She put thousands of miles between her and her mother coming home late. She had needed her home then because she was just a child. Still, it would keep right on, Don's late nights, bringing back that feeling of fear and anxiety she used to feel waiting for her mother to come home. Abnormally high frequency of brain waves is not a nice thing and not an easy enemy to fight. Back then, the tyranny of *what-ifs* had been her bedtime routine for years. What if she doesn't come home this time? What if she is too scared this time? What if he hits her too hard? So many rows that they become the norm. So many bruises, they become less shocking each time. So many tears. A way of life. Self-pity. An endless cycle. What if he actually kills her one of these days? He didn't. But that wasn't the point either.

Meli gets up and pours herself another glass of wine. No point going to bed now. Sleep would only be full of variations on how Don would leave her. Like many times before, Meli would wake up sobbing loudly and breathless. The pain of losing him was suffocating. She had stopped grinding her teeth over the years but this sort of thing would bring it back. She hated herself for being so inadequate at being an adult. She hated herself and she hated her mother. But it hurts to hate and that's why the teeth have to grind to let the pain squeeze past.

Chapter 5

Two Sticks to Beat Yourself With

1990s - 2000s

Central London

Making her coffee in the morning, a few months later, Meli thinks about her job. She is getting sick of it. It isn't for her anymore. She wonders to herself, and later to her therapist, why she bothered to become a lawyer. She is sick of it. Sick, sick, sick. The problem with law is too much judgement, too much of right and wrong, too much black and white. Grabbing her grownup leather briefcase, throwing on her grownup woollen coat, Meli thinks about this unrealistic expectation that life should be fair and the delusion that we can make it so. The too simple duality of Defence and Prosecution, defensiveness and attack.

A defence of an attack and an attack on the defence, it was like she was part of it. It was the sum of her parts. No room for something more imaginative, some shade of creativity, thinking free from the margins of painstakingly crafted law books, full of prescription, proscription and prohibition, judging and sentencing. Getting away with it. The world made of a crime, the aggressor, the defender, the victim, judge and jury. People judging people. People good and bad. Black and white. Sometimes they tried to be more nuanced, but in the end, there were just not enough resources.

The lift opens and Raul and Michael walk in to share with her the three floors to the ground, where they will leave her to walk into Café Nero, which is right next door. Meli often thinks about how ironic it seems the café should carry the name of a man who resolved his power struggle not by sitting down with a nice cup of coffee and a good conversation, but by having his mother murdered. And was implicated in the murder of one of his five wives and his stepbrother. Perhaps it felt quite at home to the English. Nero adopted by the country as he was by his father, the Emperor Claudius.

A, 'Hi!' is exchanged. Smiles are gifted and a 'you ok?' given.

She says, 'yes, though I'm thinking I'm getting bored of being a lawyer.'

They all laugh good-naturedly and she walks off in the direction of the northern line.

Raul and Michael are in their fifties. They are fine-looking men. A happy couple, as only a couple can be when they have survived together against many odds, for thirty years sharing their lives and rarely being seen separately. They are Meli's favourite neighbours. They collect and sell Lalique glass. Their flat is like a Lalique museum, or, a shrine, depending on the way you see things.

About an hour and a few cancelled trains later, because someone assaulted someone, someone obstructed the closing door and so on, Meli gets off a bus and walks the short distance to Montague House across the Thames. This is a place where police officers accused of a crime or lesser misconduct are invited to come and explain themselves to other police officers charged with judging what is on the right side of the law and what is not. The right side seems a moveable feast. Men judging men, also women, but not so often.

'Thank you for coming so promptly,' says the male police inspector, in charge of the sensitive case Meli has been called to assist with. 'Would you like a cup of tea or coffee before we start?' Working as a criminal defence lawyer for a firm specialising in representing the police force of England and Wales has its perks. If you are representing an ordinary Joe, not a copper Joe, there will be no freshly made cups of tea or coffee available, not on your Nelly.

'Black with sugar, thank you. Is my client here?'

'Yes, I will take you through now and bring your coffee there if you like?'

'Perfect.'

Meli's client that day is a police detective. He is accused of rape. The victim says she wasn't raped. She says it in her own tongue, through a translator, words written down by another person. The words describing what happened to her, three steps removed from the act. She can't speak English.

What would she say if she could? How much can be lost in translation? Meli wonders.

The young constable on duty with the detective that day says she was. He saw it, he said. Or, maybe he heard it, he is not sure exactly, but he knew it happened. He was sickened to his stomach. He just could not believe the man he looked up to until that day could do something like that.

'He is, how shall I put it, well, he is not quite right in the head.'

'I see,' says Meli, waiting, not seeing.

They are in an interview room where they will be for many hours yet. The investigating team gave them some disclosure about the allegation, but undoubtedly held some back, some very potent bit that would undermine the entire defence if she isn't careful. But Meli is good at playing games.

'There have been a number of incidents where a few of my officers raised a concern about him. I think we will have no difficulty at all undermining his evidence and discrediting him as a witness. He is basically not quite there.'

'Sure. Shall we go back to the allegation and hear your account of the evening?'

'We went on a raid to close a brothel,' he starts. 'We were tipped off about this illegal set-up and we were going to promptly shut it down. When we got there, the girl offered her services before we closed the shop. I declined, of course. It is possible,' the detective says, 'the troubled young man heard her offer and jumped to conclusions. He wasn't there the whole time. So he couldn't have seen. The door was ajar. Why would I leave it ajar if I wanted to do that?'

Even on the detective's account, things aren't looking ethically peachy. He should never have been alone in the room with a vulnerable female, never mind leaving the door ajar. How much ajar? Just enough to prevent full sight but allow the claim why would I do that with the door open? It doesn't stack up, thinks Meli. His account is like a wonky tower that would not withstand the gentlest breeze by way of scrutiny. It wouldn't stack up to the investigators either and if they kept on asking questions, which Meli asked just once, he would incriminate himself before they knew what was what. Like when she asked why was the door ajar, with him and her in there alone. Why was he alone with her?

'So, what I think might be the best thing to do is to provide the investigating team with a statement in which you will outline your denial and offer no further comment at this stage. It will give us an opportunity to see what evidence they have and we can always provide an extra statement if necessary, although it is my feeling that will not be advisable at this stage.'

Meli wants to see who says what before she commits her client's account on the record. He would have to stick by it from then on, all the way to the trial if there is to be one. It is important he doesn't say anything in the statement that could be proved false at a later stage. That would undermine his credibility. The less he says the better. But it is always important to state the denial from the outset. Make them work hard for that conviction.

Meli used to think this. Today, when she comes off the autopilot briefly, she wonders what was the point. She is almost sure the detective is lying. She saw the girl's statement. There is stuff, tiny, incidental stuff, stuff so tiny you wouldn't bother making it up. But it tells you everything. The girl was raped, because to rape someone you don't actually need to tie them down and physically force them to perform the act. To rape someone, you need to have some kind of sex with another when the other is not truly consenting. This woman could not truly consent given all her circumstances. If consent means an actual free-will decision on desire to be intimate with someone or otherwise. The young constable is vulnerable but he is not lying and there is nothing wrong with his eyes and his ears. It will be a colossal waste of everyone's time to play out this charade and yet that is exactly what will happen.

'Absolutely, I totally agree, Meli. I think it is a great plan. Although I was thinking I could just say look I didn't do it. Ask me what you want. I am happy to go with your advice.'

Nice move, thinks Meli careful to hide her unease. He is making it look like he is only going "no comment" because she advises him to. Oh well. Perhaps he believes that. He looks like he believes himself for sure.

In an interview under caution, Meli reads out the prepared statement, denying the allegation. They will now sit tight, simply waiting to see if there is enough evidence to pursue this without him saying anything at all. It doesn't look good to not say anything. Neither will it be good to say anything. It isn't like he is going to confess. She has done this too many times.

The thing catching her eye on this grotesque fashion runway is how deeply the detective is convinced of his own lie. It is like he becomes all of a sudden detached from reality. He is sure he didn't do it.

'Meli, I really didn't do it. I need you to believe me,' he says.

He doesn't need her to believe him. He just needs her to act as if she believes him, which she will.

Months later, when they are finally told he won't be charged with a criminal offence, he thanks her, but with an indignation that only the truly culpable is capable of.

He says, 'they are going to dismiss me from the police force and I will be losing my pension for one prostitute who illegally came to this country when I have a loving wife and three small children who have to go through this grief. Where is the justice in that?'

In this moment, he forgets his mum and dad also entered this country in dubious and complex circumstances. Just as in a previous moment, not that long in the past, he forgot he had a wife and three small children when he behaved like a predator, a tiger on a prowl. Righteous ape, silverback leader, he believes all females on his territory belong to him. But, the leaders can become losers and can end up banished not only from power but from the troupe altogether.

'Sometimes, justice is imperceptible,' she says, non-committal enough, and then she has a call to take. She won't have to shake his hand.

Some days later, eating their dinner together, Meli says to Don, she feels a bit sick thinking about it.

She says, 'an ordinary man would have gone to prison for this.'

Don says, 'Although, another ordinary man might have just paid an ordinary woman for her business and not be accused of rape, right?'

Meli thinks about this for a while and then says 'the ordinary woman would, in both cases, be fucked. She would be illegal and fucked. And that's not right. Neither of those things is right because if she wasn't illegal, she might not have to be fucked to earn a living. And don't give me the, "it could be her choice." She is an immigrant who doesn't speak English.'

'Hm.' Don has no more to say on this. His view is not to think about things you can't change.

Later, they go to bed lost in their thoughts but lost together, and then in the morning, Meli feels sick again.

She thinks, could it be.

First, there are two lines on the stick. Don says, 'fuck' but he smiles and hugs her tight and Meli feels like she might burst with happiness. There is so much love inside her, for the world, for him, for the tiny mixture of chromosomes inside her. She is happy. Maybe for the first time, she is very completely happy.

And then, two months later, there is a lot of blood and some bits of something that was once promising to be a living thing. And the pain in her abdomen that tells her it is over.

Miscarriages do happen just like that. Often for no reason other than a random collection of biological variables.

Chapter 6

Eliza's Apology

2020

London, outside of the M25.

'Well, I was just going to apologise but now I don't want to.' Eliza moves her head from left to right in overdramatised indignation, completely incongruent with her age or cultural background. This is a move she learned on some You-Tube programme. In her head, she hears Eliza respond, *no, I didn't, you can't blame everything on You-Tube, mum,* and she chooses not to have this conversation out loud. Meli knows that Eliza wants to apologise but she is worried Meli doesn't want her apology. So she rejects Meli before Meli can reject her apology. But this one is still a conversation Meli has to have with her.

'I don't want your apology, Eli. They are becoming meaningless.'

'I see. So shall I just never apologise when I do something?' She doesn't say 'something wrong', just 'something'. She just can't. Don would say she is your daughter. But she is so much more, Meli knows.

'No. That is not what I said. Did I say, Eli, you should never apologise when you do something wrong?'

'No. But you said it was meaningless, which is basically saying don't apologise.'

'No. I did not say apologising is meaningless. What I said was your apologies are becoming meaningless, referring to this very specific situation and I think you know this. You are just determined to keep fighting me.' Meli is a honing steel to Eliza's knife, but she doesn't say that. She gets sharper every day. 'Apologising for the same thing you keep on doing over and again doesn't have any meaning.'

'So, if I should only apologise when I mean it and never do the thing again I will have to be a perfect child who never does anything naughty?' Eliza is outraged at this massive inconvenience.

Meli suppresses a smile.

Eliza a hawk, sensing her mother's moment of weakness is now in a groove. 'Which basically means you are asking me to never have fun again because if you never do anything naughty you never have fun, obviously. Because most actually fun things are a bit naughty.'

'I see what you are saying. You have a point. But that is not what we are talking about right now.'

'Err, yes, we just are, Mum. You started this argument because you didn't want my apology.'

'No. This argument started because you wanted to have your cake and eat it.'

'Stop doing this.'

'Doing what?'

'You know what you are doing. You are saying things. I don't know what they mean and then you distract me.'

'You wanted us to have a nice long bedtime when we talk

about our day and we listen to some meditation and you read and then I stay with you until you fall asleep.'

'Yes.' Eliza says suspiciously. 'And?'

'And? And you wanted to watch that You-Tube video, which I said was going to take up the time which we had to do all those things so you had to decide between what you wanted more. It was one or the other.'

'I didn't hear you say that.' Eliza offers, lying, waiting and seeing if she will get away with it. This is in fact where the argument started. Meli reacted to Eliza's obvious lie by shouting, which Eliza was prompt to point out. 'And then you started shouting.'

'Yes, and I shouldn't have but I was reacting to what I believed was you lying.'

'So now you are calling me a liar.'

'Is that what I am doing?'

Eliza detects the changed tone in her mother's voice. She has always been so perceptive. In a split second she goes from ferocious to fluffy and she says, 'Mum, are you ok?' So much softness in her voice it threatens to overwhelm. Why does kindness always feel like hazardous material? Highly flammable acts of kindness, that's how they feel to Meli.

She is suddenly tired. She feels old. She looks at Eliza and says, 'I am ok, love, are you ok?' She remembers life is short and she so loves to kiss her daughter's cheeks, and then she does and she says, 'I love you Eli.'

'I love you more, Mum, triple dibs.'

They didn't resolve it. Meli lets her get away with it to an extent. To the extent that Eliza knows that Meli let her get away with it but she also knows that Meli was right and she was wrong. Meli never had conversations like this with her mother. That has to be something at least.

Chapter 7

Don is Hoovering

2020

London, outside of the M25.

Don is hoovering. They recently bought a new hoover, one of those lightweight, cordless, clever things. Don admires a good bit of engineering and he will enjoy it even if it is only designed to pick dirt up from the floor. Also, it is easy to enjoy something if you haven't done it before, thinks Meli, but she does not mind this too much. Evolution takes time and it comes in mysterious ways.

'This is so smart,' Don says to Meli, beaming with pleasure at this technological miracle, as he switches it off with one smooth touch of a finger. 'Ta-daa!'

'The hoover? Yes, darling. Amazing. It hoovers.' She smiles at him, as she says it and he grins in return, a sparkle in his eye. Just a little moment in a day, that is all they have for each other, most of these days, days of being parents, playing responsible adults. They only have two children but it often feels like twenty. Their needs and demands are like octopus tentacles with their infinite degree of freedom, constantly on the move. Six arms, two legs, three hearts and nine brains. It is a lot of limbs to stop from breaking and a lot of heart to keep filled with goodness and protect from ache. And you can't always.

Moments like these, when they share something that is unspoken, are like dates, a date over a hoover. Some have trees with forbidden fruit and some have hoovers. It's a date that will have to last until the next moment that sustains their limbs and their heart's desire for more.

'I might get the smaller handheld one of these too, you know,' Don says.

'Is this foreplay?' she replies, her eyes laughing.

Chapter 8

The Tooth Fairy

2020

London, outside of the M25.

It is an evening after a long day. Today, Meli has seen eight clients. It is a lot of stories to hear and to hold in one day. Meli is getting ready for bed, thinking about one of them in particular. He sometimes makes her think of her Burt. He's a young Syrian man, who came to this country when he was eight, a bit younger than Burt is now. Separated from his mum, he crossed the seas with his father. They were escaping something, in the hope of finding something better. That's why his mum agreed to it. Meli's head comprehends while her heart beats hard and fast, confused at this atrocious truth. How could you be in search of a better life while being separated from a mother who loves you?

Meli used to feel guilty for not seeing her children all day. This one day in the week which she had cut out from all the other days in the week to be something else than a mum for one whole day. No breakfast time with them, no dinner together.

She doesn't feel guilty anymore. The fact of the matter is you never stop being a mum. They are always in your head, or at least, never too far from it. Anything can call them up in an instant. Like an invisible umbilical cord, it gets a tug any time, no warning.

Meli is thinking about this young Syrian man, boy, really, who was telling her earlier today about sleeping on the floor of an unfurnished house when they first arrived in the UK. When his school friends saw it, they mocked him and told everyone. Kids can be cruel, you can say that again. Meli walks into Burt's room. She needs to tuck him in. Kiss his warm, soft cheek. He is growing every day. He is an outline of a young man, more than a boy now. She sits on the edge of the bed, watching him breathe, inhaling his innocence. She finds these moments so sustaining. Her children, her life source. How could you send your child away? What sustains you then? How long is the umbilical cord?

Burt takes himself to bed these days. Bedtimes with him have always been much easier, quieter, more serene than with Eliza. He has always been ready to switch off when night fell. He would fall asleep so fast, as quick as he could say *Mum I will never fall asleep tonight.*

Then Meli remembers that time, not that long ago, when he insisted she tell him the truth about the tooth fairy. She had been trying to circumvent this one for a while. That night he was imploring relentlessly and he wouldn't let it drop. Meli was tired that night too. Something in her was giving in and he knew so he kept on. Did she want him to know? Was it selfish of her to tell him?

She asked him would it not make him feel sad if she was to say to him the tooth fairy wasn't real.

And he said, 'no,' and then, 'I don't know,' in a small voice.

And then, he said, 'so she isn't real. I knew it!'

Meli felt so sad. She could not say it out loud like that. Bursting bubbles. It felt so horrible.

The next night Burt had hugged her. He cried and he said it did make him feel sad to know the truth. Meli felt like a failure. Once again she didn't trust her judgement. She told him because someone said you can't lie to them, or was it because she was tired. She couldn't tell anymore. Someone said to her they will find out sooner or later and imagine how betrayed they will feel when they find out you kept telling them a lie. Meli wanted to say, *but it is not a lie. It is a story. We all need stories.*

The thing about stories is they are open to as many interpretations as there are people telling them. Meli tasted the familiar taste of her tears. 'I am sorry Burtie,' she whispered. 'I am sorry that the tooth fairy is not real.'

Chapter 9

Sleeping Beauties

1980s-1990s

A small town in a little country

They are barely seventeen and they are barely dressed, some of them, anyway. Meatloaf blares out of the girls' room radio, the dorm a beehive, buzzing with hormones, dreams and hopes. Brood chambers for desires crushed and remade, daily.

Tania is now blonde. Betty is not spotty anymore. She is still completely flat-chested. Meli feels for her because she herself is only a bra-size away, if she bothered wearing bras. It is unclear to Meli why she feels deprived, somehow cheated out of a good bargain with her b-size cup. Why should it matter to anyone what size breast women have? Why is it a thing? A thing for men to think and talk about and a thing for women to worry about, one way or another. Too big, too small, too whatever, like their breasts are an object for someone else's pleasure or otherwise. It really pisses her off. And yet here she is feeling sorry for Betty, doing the same thing, presuming Betty cares about it in the same way. But what if she didn't?

Well, that would be awesome. Still, Meli doubts it. Tanya has been indiscreet about this to Gabi, and obviously Gabi told Meli. But even she if didn't, Meli doubts it is possible to not take in, get swept up by, the undercurrent chatter of the other's expectations, already woven into the fabric of their society. The cloth is cut as soon as they start telling stories to their little kids. They will all wear it, but like the emperor's invisible cloth, they will be blind to their own internalised misogyny.

They are like the Sleeping Beauties waiting to be woken up by their prince. Has anyone ever seen a flat-chested Sleeping Beauty? They're stories of what men want, or like, when it comes to choosing the one, stories about women who are snide about each other, compete crudely, unkindly, like Cinderella's sisters, when they need to make themselves feel a part of something, to be chosen. And what is the mother's role in all of this? Has she bought into it? Could she not? She did go to work, and she certainly never read *any* stories to Meli. Meli had a working mother, a mother who could not cope with many things in life. And her way of managing was to drink it away, drink away the feelings of insecurity, the overwhelming incompetence at being a grown up. You could easily drink your life away if you weren't careful.

Sure there are other stories about women too, but Meli is fairly certain the history of folklore favours men's desire over women's. Thus she is going to have to be a bit more like them, the men. If you can't beat them and all that. Returning her mind to her dorm room, Meli thinks about Martina, who is dangling her head down from her bed, the lucky one, with a perfect shoe fit. She is the first one in the room with a serious boyfriend. The unspoken envy of her roommates slithers around the room like an angry snake stripped of its venom.

Gabi is still Thelma to her Louise, and they carry on playing, still in search of the meaning of life, and a boyfriend. They are definitely not sleeping or beauties, but they are making their own ball every day, as they learn to sort out the seeds from the ashes.

'Have you found it today?' says a girl from the room next door, as Meli walks through the small hallway that joins the two rooms. It is a joke that all the girls in their class are in on. It's hard not to when you shared one space for two years, all thirty-six of you. Privacy is not a thing in nunneries. Maybe that's why they chatted to God so much. But Communism, their country's new god, took care of that. Religion was suspended, until further notice. Privacy is also not a thing at boarding school dorms. Nor, it seems to Meli, is it highly valued.

'Not yet. Let you know when I do.' Entering her room, closing the door, the room silent as Calypso's cave. All wait for their turn to have a moment with their Odysseus.

Meli climbs into her bunkbed, opens up the textbook and starts reading. Soon she says what they always say. 'Does anyone have anything to eat? I really need something to keep going. This chapter is threatening to be How to kill your reader by too much to highlight case study.' Meli likes highlighting, but not too much, maybe twenty percent of the text. Most of the time, twenty percent is all you need. Gabi is chewing on her nails. They are forever running out of food. All their allowance goes on wine, coffee and cigarettes.

Tania puts her head down non-committedly and Betty says, 'Sorry no.' But that isn't true.

'You bobbly cow,' says Gabi, 'I just saw you push that packet of cheese balls under your pillow.'

Tania shrugs, and swallows and Betty says, 'Well, you shouldn't have spent all your money on fags and wine, how about that?'

Gabi rolls her eyes and says, 'Thanks, Mum'.

Meli gets herself off her bunk and says, 'let's go see if Gita will give us something from the kitchen?' Gita is a cook in the dorm's kitchen. Gita is also Tom's mum, and Tom is a boy who would very much like to give Gabi food or *anything* she wants and more, if she dares to want.

'Chances are,' Meli says, 'if there is something, Gita will be kind.'

'It will give someone the wrong idea,' says Gabi, weighing it up, someone getting the wrong idea later versus food now.

'Or the right idea?' Meli, raising her eyebrows, forming a question mark with her face as she does.

Gabi goes red. 'Shut up, Meli. We're not all brave like you,' she says, climbing down from her top bunk.

'I know,' says Meli matter-of-factly, grabbing her handbag and putting her arm around Gabi's shoulder in a conciliatory way. 'But, I'll be there, right beside you, I promise.'

'Please don't,' says Gabi, still pretending to be mad at Meli. The door slams behind them, loudly like an exclamation mark.

'That should have annoyed Betty,' Meli says, with a small grin. They wander in the direction of the kitchen, arms linked, and something smells good.

They do almost everything together. A few weeks later, Gabi will have her first time, while Meli will be next door. Playing cards with Tom's brother.

Chapter 10

The Tale of Sexy Witches

1980s-1990s

A small town in a little country

Martina's head emerges from behind her book, closing it with 'God, this is so dull.' She sounds completely indifferent to what she is saying. It is some skill Martina has, to look like she is not interested in her own words.

Betty doesn't look up, just sighs heavily. She is worried about their psychology test the next day. She is taking things too seriously, thinks Meli.

Meli would struggle to ever understand why people would take things seriously. She says so, adding, 'I just don't see it myself. Nothing ever lasts as far as I can tell, good or bad, and everything you love or hate is eventually going to be gone, one way or another. What is the point of taking anything seriously? Life is too short to be serious.'

In answer to this, some subconscious contribution to the conversation, Martina gets in a position. She started this new practice of dangling her head down from the top bunk in order to make her hair go naturally curly. It seems to Meli to be a pretty fucking unnatural way to go about it but as Martina now has a serious boyfriend everyone lets it pass.

Meli asks Martina, 'is this you saying the world is better seen upside down? Giving us another perspective?'

Betty grunts. She is not interested in philosophy. Life may be short but she is going to be in control of hers. And in order to be in control, you have to know stuff, be good at stuff, pass exams, study hard, go to university, that kind of thing. Betty doesn't believe in twenty percent. Meli with her philosophy is not going to get very far, or if she does, it will be all random. And Betty is not about to take any random chances. For her, life is too long for that.

Martina says, 'You should try it.'

'I don't like my hair looking natural though,' says Meli. She sleeps with metal curlers in her hair. It is not comfortable, but was Marilyn's life? You can't have it all. You certainly can't be a natural Marilyn.

Gabi in her top bunk with the textbook, frowning, not understanding, memorising. Meli feels disappointed with the day. Nothing exciting happened and now it sure won't. Everyone was serious and no one wanted to play. And Meli likes playing. It makes her feel something. Nothing exciting ever came out of being serious. She doesn't know it yet, but this is Meli's starting point to feminism.

'Meli, you better take a look at this fucking thing,' Gabi warns. That was one of Gabi's things, to warn Meli. 'It's a lot to read. That bloody weasel scares the jiggering bells out of me.' Gabi sometimes uses words that belong to the dialect of her village, which is hardly spoken outside of it, and in the unlikely event it is uttered, it is never understood. Which, at their age, makes the dialect crass except that Gabi somehow makes it sound hilarious.

'Why,' says Betty from the other side's top bunk, 'she's only tiny.'

'She looks like an angry gnome. That's just not natural for a woman.'

'Is it natural for a man?' Meli asks.

'If you ask me,' says Gabi, 'one hundred percent. How many of the seven dwarves you know were women? None that I know of. At least with a man you know where he belongs in the story. The weasel is a gnome anomaly. Plain wrong.'

'Don't say if you ask me.' Meli says.

'She could be a witch. She has a wart on her face.' Tania chips in, adding as the thought occurs to her, 'She often munches on apples, come to think of it.'

'Yeah but she doesn't look like a witch, does she. Witches are kind of sexy, in a witchy sort of way. She just looks like an angry gnome.' Gabi is not letting go.

Betty looks up now. 'Did you say sexy witches?'

Upside down Martina says, 'Yeah, I can see it.' Her eyes look weird upside down.

They are all laughing now and no one is learning a thing, except maybe a thing or two about witches. These are the moments that Meli will one day remember and think, this was the thing, to just sit and be in company, with friends, sharing an ordinary moment, when you know you are lucky, because you feel light in your heart and you are laughing, and you are playing, just like a child, but this time with words and thoughts not dolls or Johny Deer. But it is a story of a moment you can't retell properly. You can't share it and you can never have that same moment again but you also have that moment forever. It is you had to be there type of a thing.

'Gabi, what the fuck are jiggering bells?'

Chapter 11

Busted not Bust

1980s-1990s

A small town in a little country

It's Sunday night and Meli is hanging out of the window having a cigarette. Martina is huffing and puffing because of the smell but doesn't say anything because she knows this is an emergency break. Meli had a bad weekend at home. The girls can tell as soon as Meli walks into the room with Gabi. No jokes, no playing. Something is up. But they will wait until Meli is ready to talk about it. No privacy but solidarity, yes.

'Meli! Meli! Matron's coming!'

The door opens just in time for Tania to say this, slipping into her bed and switching off the night light. She is late to the room because she is sick. Tania is dabbling with drugs. Meli has actually been a bit worried about Tania, which will turn out to be prescient. Tania will eventually end up in a mental health institution, locked up against her will, her children taken away from her, but for now, youth experiencing drugs was the least of Meli's problems. This moment in time could be her own undoing.

Recently, her form tutor intercepted a letter from a friend which was full of colourful language. The interception wasn't an act of high perception or anything as the envelope was covered in red lipstick kisses and a picture from Dirty Dancing. Not the one of the sensible older sister singing the polite song.

The interception may also have gone marginally better had Meli not decided to challenge her tutor for opening the letter. In front of the whole class, Meli suggested the tutor had no right to open their private correspondence. Bold move. This is a country where foreign travel still feels a bit like an incestuous taboo. Her tutor went so pale with rage she looked like she might white out. She stormed out of the class instead. The next Meli heard, they had a meeting to discuss her expulsion. Her PE tutor, supported by their literature tutor, who wore bright red, flowy, corduroy skirts and also liked Meli, suggested this was ridiculous. Good thing about life is that if you just have a few people who like you, even if you have many more who don't, with a bit of luck, you will be ok. Meli wasn't expelled. But now, with the cigarette situation, Meli doesn't want to think about this.

'Right!' Says the matron. 'I will stand here until one of you tells me who did this.' Lucky again, this matron knows who did it. Her nose is red but the girls don't see it as they all pretend to be asleep. What a pantomime. Everyone knows that no one is sleeping. Everyone knows that matron knows that and everyone knows that everyone knows who was smoking. Meli's luck is that matron also has problems and she solves them with a secret glass of wine or two. On or off duty makes no difference to a woman whose life is falling apart in front of her eyes. She stands there for a couple of minutes, which feel like hours, and then shuts the door never to say a word about it.

Meli does. She says 'thanks' to the silence of the room and then Martina exhales so deeply as though she has been holding her breath the whole time and says 'fucking hell' and she never swears and they all burst out laughing. They can't believe what Meli just got away with. Adrenaline can be a fun thing. Just not too much, maybe twenty percent.

It is coming up to their A-levels week. A week of exams. They have a week off school in order to revise. Everyone is serious. Including Meli. Just for this week. She is secretly quite excited. She won't admit this to anyone, not even Gabi, but she loves exams. It's a chance to prove some people wrong, which is always fun, people like the weasel. She learns all four years' syllabus that week. She is going out with a bang.

They are eighteen and they are about to close the door on their dorm rooms for the last time. It will be bitter and it will be sweet. The bewitching Siren sings the ballad of the promised adulthood inexorably drawing them out and away.

Her head heavy in Shakespeare, Meli gets roused out of her reading stupor by the tannoy calling her to the matron's office. There is a phone call for her.

This is not good. No one ever calls the dorm with good news. Good news can always wait.

Chapter 12

Who is It in The Mirror Looking Back at You?

1990-2000

Central London

'Meli,' Don says as he puts a coffee on her bedside table with a gentle clank. Just like him.

'I'm sorry, I'm not here right now,' noise, from under her pillow.

'It's nice outside.' He opens the curtains to prove it.

She can feel the light flood the room even with her head buried under the mass of down and feather. 70/30. The light is an unwelcome visitor. It didn't call to say it would be coming. She wouldn't have answered.

'Shall we go for a walk?'

'Don't feel like it,' adding, 'sorry.' Don was trying so hard to make everything normal again. Don the Normaliser. Why did people insist on making things normal. There was so little normal about how she felt right now.

'Still, shall we go?' He opens the windows to let air in. Another intruder. How much more of this ambush of normality can she withstand?

'Maybe later.' She is not interested in light, in air. She just wants to go back in time when she could put her hand on her abdomen and feel life brewing under it.

'Meli.'

'Yes.'

'You will have to get out of this room one of these days.'

'Why?'

Alarmed at the idea, Meli lets her mind wander to the night before. Did she make any promises to get out? She remembers she decided it was time to resign. It still makes sense in the morning. Phew, she thinks, should have done it ages ago. Don is supportive although he is probably other things too. Sipping on a glass of red wine, curled up by the burning fireplace, she wrote her letter of resignation last night. She might need to rewrite it. She wonders if she cares enough though and also why does she always have to doubt herself, her words, and her thoughts. Why do they need tweaking so much? It was like her words carried some charge, like they could cause damage, like she was always shooting from the hip and then frantically trying to close the stable door with the horse bolted. It seems so silly, how people go on living their lives like someone is watching. They all behave motivated by seeking something from *outside* of themselves, someone else's approval or disdain, applause or scolding, punishment or a reward. How many stickers did you get today? Who was the Star of the Week? It's like they had no autonomy to be who they really were, like who they were depended on what others thought of them.

It's like they don't know who they are. They never dare to find out. Instead they shape themselves in the mould of an image assigned to them by someone they cared about. She was always sporty. He was always going to be an achiever. He never was an academic, unlike his brother. There. Just like that. Their story is shaped before they have any say in it.

'Thanks for the coffee.' Meli says. She needs to go to the loo. She will have to get up. It's frustrating how the physical needs interfere with the psychological ones. Sometimes bodies just insist on living even when minds feel dead.

'Raul and Michael are going to call later this evening. They wondered if you fancied going over to theirs, for New Year's Eve.'

Meli is silent for a while. 'But you know I don't fancy anything at the moment. You could have just told them that.'

'No. You can tell them that.'

Don is frustrated too. He likes people and their company. He likes living his life. He doesn't spend too much time on setbacks. He really wants Meli to be more like that too, more rational, grown up. Except it increasingly seems to Meli people don't really tend to grow up. They grow bigger, yes, up, not so much. It is like there is some unspoken universal conspiracy to carry on role-playing adults like they did as kids. They're playing mums and doctors and robbers and policemen. Role-playing adults who are not kids anymore is different to playing as adults. One is a farce, the other, art. When you play as an adult it's called being creative – you create a painting, or a sculpture or a book. You design a beautiful garden or a beautiful piece of furniture. Meli recently went to see an exhibition by a Portuguese artist called Paula Rego. It was stunning. It was absurd and yet it was the real life. Real life is quite absurd. On the other hand, role-playing adults are tedious to watch, like bad theatre, but it is harder still for Meli to take any part in it other than as a bystander, the audience. She's on the outskirts, observing, occasionally getting pulled in. Not for too long. They even made costumes for themselves. The lawyers put on their wigs, dressing up in Harry Potter gowns. Bankers in their spick and span suits and mums and dads drink alcohol like a badge of honour. They sometimes smoke cigarettes and yell at their children, having lost their sense of humour. Or, they drink herbal teas and eat kale, call their kids darling and wrap their presents in a paper which matches the balloons, saying things like, "absolutely fabulous". It sounds more like fe-bulous. Meli has decided to opt out. Staying in bed seems preferable. She doesn't feel like playing. Doesn't feel like playing a stupid New Year's Eve game either.

'And I'll tell you another thing I can't do. I can't keep on doing this,' Don says.

'What? Grieving?'

'Yes. I don't want to be swallowed by it. You act like you do.'

'I am not acting.'

In the end, it will take two more months. During these, Meli writes a book. She calls it *I Am Not Here Right Now*. It's an outpouring, an orgy of hurt feelings. They are coupling and multiplying. It's a frenzied dance she is dancing. She feels exhausted, but she keeps on writing and it ends up being 170,000 words. That is a lot of words that had to come out of her. Meli is sitting on a bench in Bunhill Fields Burial Ground, on 38 City Road, when she finishes it. She closes the book and she knows it is time. Things have a way of organically passing. They call it time healing but it is more like a scar tissue formation. The original trauma can be still seen if looked at closely and the skin will never go back to what it was before. So, it is not healing, not really. It is more like enduring.

The night before she returns to work, writing a new letter of resignation, much shorter, it occurs to Meli she can sum up the three months of her life in a paragraph. And then she sees it. It was just that. It was a paragraph in her life. And now it was time to go back to her story. Back to where she left off. Her story did not end here.

It was true all things came to an end, not just the good and the bad things, but also the things in between. The things, the processes, that connect things together, that tie them like an invisible link to make a whole. It's a bridge between two states of mind, between two paragraphs, one about a despair and an end of something, the other, the new beginning. It was time to hop back on this rumbustious horse. You have to get back on when you get thrown otherwise you might never get to ride again. And what kind of life is that.

For some reason, she remembers Emma. She phoned her on the day she was walking through this same ground, when seemingly apropos of nothing she could discern with her conscious mind, her legs carried her over to a bench. Her hands, acting all alone, found the phone, her mouth found the words and Emma heard her. She said, 'why don't you take some time out?'

That was three months ago. Often, at the end of things, we remember their beginning.

Chapter 13

Office Politics

1990-2000

Central London

Meli is in the office. It is her last day. She was going to work out a three months' notice, but Heather and Matthew ask her why she doesn't leave earlier, under all the circumstances. Heather and Matthew are her employers. All the circumstances being Meli is pregnant again. They are also that she miscarried previously and that it might be a good idea for her to have the least stressful pregnancy possible. It makes sense. How nice of them.

But Meli can't take a gift. Behind all gifts lurks a suspicion. They must think she is a liability. That she is unstable. Too vulnerable. That she used them and then ditched them without appreciating what they did for her. Not repaying their kindness. There is a lot of this going on in her head.

Don said, 'who cares. Let's look ahead. There is a lot to look at there.'

But Meli is looking back. Her bosses are a couple. A

faint glimmer of something familiar makes her feel a bit lightheaded. Why is she ascribing all of these thoughts to them? Are they really theirs, or do they belong some other place? Is there someone else out there who feels she is a liability? That she is unstable? After all she left her country without saying a goodbye to her own parents before she turned nineteen. Too vulnerable. A highly flammable adolescent. The self-accusations are too familiar. She used them and then ditched them without appreciating what they did for her. All her life. Oh God, what is wrong with her? Stop. Stop. Stop. Return your head to the office, Meli, this is where the rest of your body is.

'Hi, Meli!' says her colleague, Kate, walking into the office, which they share. Too cheerful, Kate is carrying her stomach a long way ahead of her. She is eight months pregnant. This is how pregnant Meli would have been with the Bean. It is hard to look at Kate. She is glowing. She is so happy. Meli feels so small for her envy, which is almost a thing of its own. It is visceral and it feels it has a life completely independent of her own mind or self. It is an ugly thing and Meli beats it into a corner, shut up, shut up, shut up. We now have our own growing again.

'Hey!' She forces some cheer into her tone. 'How are you feeling?'

'Oh you know, heavy,' Kate says, smiling, while carefully lowering herself into her chair like a crane with precious cargo. No, I don't, thinks Meli, I don't know.

'Excited?' Kate asks, referring to Meli's last day in the office.

Meli says, 'I think so,' and, 'I think I am going to do that course in classical history.'

'Oh, that's brilliant!' Kate says, too excited.

'Yes, I actually signed up for it. It's a three-year course so it should keep me busy while I'm not working and being a mum.

Should give me some more options on what to do later. I don't think I will ever be back to law.'

'I'm so jealous,' says Kate.

Snap! Thinks Meli.

Kate is a nice girl. Meli would never tell her how she felt about Kate's glow and happiness. She doesn't need to. Kate knows. She has been there before. She lost her first pregnancy too. Sometimes, often, women know what other women feel. And it is hard for Kate to go on pretending she doesn't. The day can't be over soon enough for either of them.

Chapter 14

One Of Those Things

2020

London, outside of the M25

When Meli did her training to become a psychotherapist, one of the things that much was made out of was that nothing was what it seemed. Au contraire, my friend, if a thing seemed one thing, most likely it was entirely another thing. Say you say, *I definitely don't mind, you decide.* The truth is that you couldn't mind more and you really want to make the decision yourself. Or, when you say: *I don't hate him!* Beware, there is a part of you that does so, very much. Another one is: *of course, I love my parents.* Err, yes and no. And so on. It's not so much the gradation, to say, *I was a bit annoyed,* may be quite a true reflection. But an absolutist statement like: *I don't get annoyed, I never get angry, he always does this, I never get to*? Nope. Have you been declared exempt of an array of human emotions? No. The spectrum is as broad as the universe but you got stuck on it somewhere, between your front door and the corner shop, with your *he always'* and *it nevers* and if you don't go back you can't go forward. You will be stuck in a position where things will forever happen *to* you and you will never end up happening.

The other thing that got said a lot was that the therapist needs to be a blank canvass. Blank canvass, neutral stance, not getting pulled into the world of her clients, but watching it. She must painstakingly watch from the right distance. Not too far, not too close. Free for the patient to project their thoughts and feelings on, is the only way this can work. They cannot know a thing about you, because if they do, it will interfere with their freedom of projection. This is the best way you can get to the heart of how they relate in the world, to the people in their worlds. Meli now doesn't think that such complete anonymity of the therapist's humanness or humaneness always works and she is ok with this. Rules are important but they shouldn't be prohibitive of thought. There are many who disagree and that is ok too. Thankfully, they don't live in 1984 anymore, right?

But, in Meli's head, 1984 is very much woven into the present through her past. Sometimes, you get away from things in real, outside life, but in your head, they are still fighting. And in your head, they are still scared little children.

When people come to see Meli, they always have a story they need to tell and this story can take years to tell. They often don't know this and, instead, they think they have come to tell her about a thing that eventually pushed them over the edge. They think if they can just figure out this bit, this latest catastrophe, everything will go back to normal. Back to normal, just like one of those things, is one of those things that doesn't exist. But it isn't what they have really come to tell. That bit, that last straw is only the ending of the first chapter. It is like a cliff-hanger. The story could go in many directions from now on.

It is by retelling the story from the beginning that the person will be able to take the ownership of how it goes next. They must go back to the beginning, to see for the first time how the jigsaw pieces fit together, how they cause each other, how one comes because of the one before and because of all the other ones around it. In the retelling, the story's characters emerge for the first time for the person to see how they all weave their story together. In the hearing of themselves telling will lie the key to their next chapter. These stories, they can now consciously inhabit, when previously they had been cast in a role without really knowing the director, actor or the play. If they listen carefully, together and long enough, a meaning will emerge. And with it, the story will become their own.

Burt has a story to tell when he gets in the car at school pick-up today. Meli can tell it is not going to be a good story. At first she thinks it will last until they get home. Burt doesn't usually consider his feelings to be a thing for public display. Any feelings. But as she is about to start up the car, Meli catches his face in the mirror and this makes her get out of her seat and go and sit next to him. She holds him close and says 'what's wrong, Love.'

Burt lets the tears unfurl on this face she loves so much. This face that's changing into a man's face. It seems a world ago when this was a little squidgy baby Burt face and it also feels like yesterday. There is no time in the world that can pass which would make her not feel like it was yesterday. It's that kind of love. But now, her baby's face distorts in that way which turns a mother into a tiger, growling, claws out, fierce and merciless, and you need strong hands and a halter to tether your heart. Meli needs to jump this one instead. No clawing.

Burt had a thing at school with a boy from his class. The boy is part of a group Burt likes to play with.

'No one likes me and no one wants to play with me and they were all running away from me like they were playing "it," but he said no one was playing, they were just running away from me because no one wants to play with me.' It's all coming out, all jumbled, like his emotions, between the tears. His nose is running tears too.

What a big ugly bully, but just a bull to her lioness, Meli's heart suddenly a hunter, fight not flight. It fills her with so much rage she could light a fire with one snap of her fingers. But this fire will have to be smouldered because she has to help Burt to process this hurt, using her words, so they can become his words, her good words.

'Why did he say that, Burtie?'

'Dunno.'

'Was he upset about something?'

'He didn't seem upset, he was laughing when he run away. Actually, no, that is not the right word. He was smirking.' Burt corrects himself. He recently learned the meaning of the word.

'Oh, Burtie. I am so sorry.' Holding him tight. 'Sometimes, when people don't feel good about themselves, they have to make other people feel bad too. It is the only way they can help themselves feel better.'

'Why doesn't he feel good about himself, Mum?'

'I don't know, Burtie. There can be a lot of reasons why people end up feeling bad inside and then they have to be mean to get it out of themselves, making others feel bad as they do it.'

'Like what reasons?'

Burt wants an answer. He needs something to hang this onto to make sense of it. He is making jigsaw pieces to put around this one. If they don't get this right enough, his jigsaw story will take on an ugly turn. He is the piece that doesn't fit, a picture now with a discrepancy, showing there is something wrong with him. That he is not good enough, somehow, to be in the picture, he, not this other boy. Burt is on the spectrum and that complicates things. Meli is on the spectrum and that complicates things too.

'Sometimes it can be because it is what they see other people do, Burtie, people they care about, people they think know better than them and they think it is best to copy what they do. Or, sometimes, it is because someone else is doing that to them. Maybe an older sibling.'

'But he doesn't have an older sibling,' says Burt.

'No. He doesn't,' says Meli.

And she is thinking about the boy's parents and how they treat other parents in the school community with disdain concealed behind smiles so superficial that the face looks cracked in asymmetry, dead eyes devoid of any warmth or realness and that deluded sense of triumph in the game of Have(s) and Have-not(s). This game means so much to them that it defines who they are. It is sad, thinks Meli. They are the sum of what they have. To have is to have an identity. The more you have, the more you are. At the school gate, picky who they talk to, who they look at even, they zoom in on those like them, recognising each other with the code of smirking, with their secret boring little conversations about nothing, about their newest Have. How do you say this to a ten-year-old boy, who thinks very literally and to whom things do not have many shades. He is just doing what he sees his parents do, Burtie, she doesn't say.

'Mum, can we email Mrs Grinchwood? To tell her?'

Mrs Grinchwood is the head of the school's Middle Department and she has been at the school at least two decades longer than Meli thought anyone should be safely exposed to too many children in one space at the same time.

'What a great idea, Burtie. We will do that first thing when we get home.'

'Can we have an Oreo as the first thing, Mum?'

'We must.'

Unlike Meli, Mrs Grinchwood, despite what her name might suggest, knows how to talk to all sorts of people's children and this is an excellent plan. Meli feels so pleased that Burt doesn't worry about telling. She also feels relieved. She needs help here. This piece of the puzzle needs to be framed correctly.

After more than one Oreo, Meli, Burt and his hurt sit down together and they write an email to Mrs Grinchwood. Sometimes, it is good to tell. At least, it feels good to say it out loud, to make yourself hear it said and to have someone mirror it back at you, your feelings, understanding. Then you feel seen and heard and the pain somehow becomes a bit less.

Burtie feels better. Meli's heart is now at a trot. She managed to jump this one. She knows she won't be able to jump them all with him. The thought can make her break out in sweat. What if he needs her and she is not there? She must stop drinking and do some exercise more regularly and not only in order to work off the calories she wishes to put back in, later in the day, much later in the day, when all the house falls silent and she climbs under the multitudinous covers and pillows in her bed, with her book, a glass of wine, and some chocolate. Probably to divert her attention with guilt, she remembers she doesn't feel this way about Eliza. With an instant effect, that makes her feel bad. It is as though Eliza, although younger, is already better equipped, like a born equestrian. But is this just a story that Meli is telling herself? Is it a story she told Eliza, without meaning to? Is Eliza just shaping herself in the mould of Meli's expectations of her? Is it something Meli did? Did she treat Eliza from the very start as though she *had* to be more independent and more quickly than her older brother? Why? Is that some unkindness?

Eliza is already a caretaker, more in tune with subtleties of unsaid things than Burt ever will be. Burt has a beautiful singing voice but does not understand tunes in conversations. There are too many sounds in one. He listens and speaks in metronome. How did this difference happen? Is this just one of those things?

When Meli sometimes got upset in front of them, it would send Burt into panic, he would become so still, as though willing himself to disappear from the field of perception. Eliza would rush over, hug her so tight it hurt, 'Mami, when you cry, it makes me want to cry. I want to take your pain away,' she said last time this happened. This made Meli snap right out of it. She did not want her daughter to feel she had to look after her. No way. She was never going to let that happen. That would be like repeating an old story of Meli's. And this was not going to happen.

'Mami, you don't need to hide when you cry,' she said another time. 'It is ok to cry in front of us. You are always telling us it is ok to cry when you are hurt or upset and to share it. You say, when you are upset and you tell someone who cares about you, it gives them a chance to say something that might make you feel better. And even if they can't say anything to make you feel better, you feel better because you don't have to hold your upset feelings like a heavy bucket all by yourself. So why don't you? Mami, please?' At the age of nine, Eliza was an incredibly human being already, as much as she was a very difficult being to argue with.

But, in the end, it is all down to the stories. We all have stories we tell ourselves about ourselves. We can't escape them.

In her story, Meli will not be like her mother. She will not make her daughter feel like she has to look after her when she herself is only a child, and she her mother.

Returning her mind to the question that has been returning like the bad smell that stays in your nostrils long after it is gone, did her children both just need her in different ways, or did she make them need her differently? Either way, "one of those things" just doesn't cut it.

Chapter 15

It Is What It Is Not

2020

London, outside of the M25

In Meli's mind, saying, 'it is just one of those things' is on the par with saying 'it is what it is.' Meli hates both in equal measure. She might have liked them once but not now. Like old socks, they have been worn out of all meaning. More than that though, they are now used to defend against thinking, or, defeat it.

She is in a session with a client who says *it is what it is* all the time. She carries it like a shield, a big, heavy, clunky shield. It weighs her down too much but she is not prepared to part from it. As long as she has it, she can fend off anything. That's what she thinks. She thinks this with that part of herself that bought into it. One of the other parts of herself is bringing her to these sessions with Meli, where she knows no thought, no paragraph of a thought can ever finish with "it's just one of those things" or "it is what it is", not that she doesn't try.

Yvonne is so desperate to please that she treats any signs of opposition or potential unpleasantness as unpalatable things you wash down with a nice cup of tea. Like the hard part of air-popped corn, indigestible, rough, scratchy facts of life, she doesn't fish them out of her mouth to examine them, even if they might choke her. Her mum popped it for her. And it would hurt her feelings. And it was ok anyway. You learn to swallow them in a way that doesn't hurt. Well, it might hurt a bit, but you get used to it. Just one of those things.

'So, I think what you are saying is that in order to protect your mum's feelings you disregard your own?'

They are talking about Yvonne having to make a decision about Christmas, Christmas dinner. It is never a straightforward equation. Meli sees it every year. Yours or mine? Theirs or ours? It seems like it should be quite easy, but it never is. Yvonne's mother will not give her options. Not really. She will make it look like she is, but it is that thing they warn you about when you start your therapeutic training. If something looks convincingly one way, it usually isn't what it seems. *So, Vons, what are we doing for Christmas this year? I really don't mind, you decide...* It is hers or hers. Yvonne really doesn't want to go, not because she necessarily doesn't want to. It would be good if she knew what she wanted herself but this has been such a long abandoned question that she doesn't even think to ask herself that. Ever. The reason she thinks she doesn't want to go is because Ewan doesn't want to go. Ewan is her new-ish boyfriend. He is in his fifties and Yvonne has taken on Ewan and his two children a few years ago, after Ewan's wife was tragically killed in a motorbike accident by Ewan's brother. You couldn't make it up.

Yvonne has no idea what she wants, so she keeps living her life wanting the things people want her to want. Ewan wants her to be a mother to his children who lost their mother far too early. Ewan also wants Yvonne to be a tidy housekeeper of his very nice house in the country. And, to be careful with the money he will give her in a monthly allowance. Which century? Meli wonders.

'I suppose,' Yvonne says, with a small smile. She feels this is a ten out of ten. Five stars. Golden badge. She is being a good girl. 'My sister and my little brother are being so difficult,' she goes on, 'as always. They have always been such a handful. Poor Mum. She doesn't have it easy. So I just try to make it a bit easier for her, you know.'

'Easier for her, harder for you,' Meli says, gently.

Yvonne is silent for a while and then says, 'It reminds me of the piano thing.'

'The piano thing,' Meli repeats. She knows this is not going to come easy but it might be coming.

'Yes. I played because it seemed to make Mum happy. I played and I played. I knew I was good at reading music. It came easy, and she was so proud of me. I couldn't understand why as this seemed such a stupid thing to be proud of, but I went along with it.'

'A stupid thing to be proud of,' Meli repeats again. Sometimes, that is all you need to do to make people hear what they are saying to themselves, being so horrible to their own self as if the own self couldn't hear it.

'Well, I didn't have to try hard. In fact, I didn't have to try at all. I just could do it, a sign, a key. Nothing original, like a copy and paste, really.'

'And being talented without having to work hard at something makes it unworthy?'

'It's not that, I don't think,' says Yvonne, 'when I see other people do it, I admire their skill but...' Yvonne trails off.

'So it is not the act of playing that is worthless. It is just you.

When *you* don't work hard, you are not worthy of praise?'

There is silence. Yvonne is looking at Meli, thinking intensely.

'In other words, you have to work hard in order to make a thing worth anything. You have to work hard to make *you* worth anything.'

Yvonne says 'that sounds odd when you put it like that, doesn't it. I don't know. Mum used to say, "you are ever such a clever girl with that piano, Vons, you will go far." I didn't go far. In fact, I didn't go anywhere. This is the furthest I have ever been. I moved a county. I hated rehearsals. Playing on repeat was not my thing. What I was good at was being thrown at the deep end. Low expectations, high returns. Reading music and getting it, straightaway. That is also why I like pub quizzes.'

Meli says nothing, waiting, just nodding and looking at the meaning between the words, the ones Yvonne is not saying, the ones she is trying to distract herself from. Words like, *I hated being a good girl*, or, *it was so hard always having to be a good girl. It made me feel so resentful of my siblings. They were free to do what they wanted.* Something like that. *I hated being in sole charge of the Keeping Mother Happy Brigade, being a one member band. I felt lonely but I seemed to have been rewarded for it. I worked hard for her love. I had to work hard to be all these things so that she would love me.* All these things Yvonne is not saying. Not yet.

'So, I ended up going to university, didn't I.' Although Yvonne is still trying to hide her accent from Meli, traces escape like little lively fireflies. It is there, threatening to break free, to take a form, to be given a lease of life. But not today. Not yet. Today, Yvonne is still in the grip of one of those things which make it what it is. Except it isn't that. And there is no going back to normal, either.

'You ended up going to university.'

'Yes. I was the only one of the siblings to do it. And I did music. Piano.' Yvonne spits it out. 'And now I am a music teacher.' She says this with so much sorrow Meli feels like hugging her. But she won't. Of course, she won't.

Instead she says, 'And that's the thing about the piano? You played it because she loved you for being good at it. And going to university, choosing piano, being the only one to go, you did all these things because it was like a security deposit on her love.'

'Yes,' Yvonne says, like she is finally found out. All crimes are a cry for help. Yvonne looks at Meli, new understanding forming as she says, 'It's like that time she took us out shopping one weekend. I pretended to enjoy it even though I absolutely hated it. I hated shopping so much. And I hated that she didn't know it. My sister loved it. She knew I hated it.'

Meli stays quiet. Yvonne is exploring how far her inner sphinx will let her push against the temple doors. She is waiting for Meli to say something. Meli does now because she knows this is hard. Very hard. Yvonne is about to reveal to herself something she has known all her life but it has been an unthought known. Something she didn't think about so she wouldn't have to know it. Her mum was not always nice. She shut those temple doors right in her face, demanding of her daughter identification with her own desires in exchange for love. She did this not knowingly, of course, but did it nevertheless. Sometimes she wasn't a good mum, definitely not the perfect mum, but she wanted Yvonne to pretend she was. She may not always have had Yvonne's best interests at heart, not that she didn't intend to. She just didn't know what was hers and what was Yvonne's.

'When your mum took you out shopping, seemingly not realising you hated it, maybe it felt like she didn't know you, really? Like with the piano thing. She didn't know things you liked or disliked.'

'Yes, now that you say that, I think it is true. I think I might have felt it at the time, a bit lonely somehow but I don't think at the time I was thinking it like that. I think I just thought I liked it.'

'Because it made her happy.' Meli says.

'Yes.'

Yvonne is quiet, waiting.

What if she did know you didn't like it, but loved *precisely* that you did it for her in the ultimate narcissistic move? She required an act of self-sacrifice of the other that felt like an act of love, but really depleted the other's sense of self to fill in the missing bit of the narcissist, Meli wants to say but doesn't. It would be too much.

'Do you think it is possible that she knew?' she says instead, because new perspectives have to be approached.

Yvonne looks up from her hands she has been picking at for the last ten minutes.

'Is it possible that she knew that you didn't like it?' Meli carries on. It has to be asked out loud. 'Like with the piano. And if she did know, then what could that mean?'

'That's why I was her favourite.' Yvonne says quietly. 'She loved me most because I put her first, because I understood she wanted me to put her first. I pretended I liked what she wanted me to like. It pleased her. It made her happy someone would do that for her.'

It was Meli's turn to be quiet.

'So that's it, isn't it?' Yvonne looks at her, shocked but liberated, 'I just went on pretending I liked things that other people like all my life, so that people might like me.'

Yvonne is crying. Meli wishes she could hug her again. But

she also knows this is better than a hug. Yvonne is on her way
to becoming Yvonne. Not Vons.

'What now?' says Yvonne to end the session.

Chapter 16

After Session

2020

London, outside of the M25

What now, indeed? Meli is feeling frazzled. Being a daughter is one of the most difficult positions she has to take up every day.

She has to call her mother. Her father is in hospital. He fell through the floor of the attic. The floors were never made secure as that part of the house was never used. Or, was it the other way round. Do you create space by using it or do you have to find a space first? Do you make it or was it there to be found? Meli used to imagine that was where their true feelings lived, up in the attic, in the dark, like ghosts. No one ever went there. They were scared what they might see. It is peculiar he went up there, looking for a picture of Dorian Gray but in reverse. Her father has always been an old man at heart.

They don't know the extent of the damage yet on her father's body or how bad the attic ghosts might look when they finally let them in. Apparently, he went up there because he was planning on doing some insulation. Don't let the ghosts in,

Dad. It's a bit late in the day for that. Meli doesn't want to speak to her mother today. She knows everything she is going to say. Unlike Yvonne, Meli didn't care about pleasing her mother. Not since she was about four years old, did she pretend to like things she didn't to make her happy. But she did much more than that. She kept her mother alive. It is a tiring thing to keep someone alive when they don't know how to live, even more so if you are a little girl doing the keeping alive.

The tone of a long-distance call is cut off after three rings. Meli would have put the phone down after the fourth.

'Halo?' says the brusque voice of her mum. She sounds alarmed as if she only expects bad news. She always sounds like that.

'Hi, Mum.'

'Oh, hello, Meli.' Relief, love, rebuke all in one tone. How does she do that?

'How is Dad?'

'Still in hospital. They operated on his leg now. It is not looking good. He will be bed bound for at least six months. I don't know how I'm going to cope.'

Meli says after a long inhale, 'I wonder how he is going to cope?' Letting it hang between them, as she exhales.

'As he does with anything, complaining and taking everything out on me.' Cold, Quiet Hate Ghost might have slipped out through the faulty insulation.

'I guess it is quite a lot to take in,' Meli says. 'He won't be able to do the most basic things for himself.' Not relenting yet. Why is everything always done *to* her mother. She probably actually believes he has done it to spite her, rendering himself immobile and dependent on her. He will be hating every moment of his life even more than he has ever done. 'Mum, I don't think he did it to annoy you. When is he allowed home?'

'On Friday,' she replies to the question, ignoring the rest.

'It will be challenging,' Meli says, 'but hopefully, with Sozanne just next door, she should be able to help out a bit.'

'Ah, that. I doubt it.' Splitting the world into good and bad, all the characters in the story of her life are goodies or badies.

'Why is that?'

' I don't know, Meli. It is a feeling I get.'

It is true that Sozanne stays very much on the outside and a good distance from the health or otherwise of Meli's parents' marriage. There were times when she could and probably should have peered in and offered something. Like the times when her brother was beating his wife black and blue, while their small child was watching, trying to protect her mum. There were other times that would have warranted an intervention but those were perhaps passable for the category of, "you don't know the whole story, best to stay out of it. It will probably come right." Sozanne was Meli's father's younger sister and she was the one he called when he fell as mother was away on some rehabilitation program out of town. Sozanne found him on the floor, gasping for breath in pain, four of his ribs broken. It hurt him to breathe, let alone talk or move. Sozanne was in shock and she said something to Meli's mother on the phone after, which felt like an accusation to her. Most things did. This is probably where her feeling came from. Her mother's attic ghosts are on a constant alert for an attack coming from her fellow ghosts at any time, from any possible where. They are a very jumpy kind, her mother's ghosts that mostly live up in the attic.

Meli stays silent just for a second longer than she should to tell her mother in this way what she can't say to her in words, which is something like, *it's on you, mum, I am not coming to rescue you this time. I am sorry. You had your whole life to leave him if that's what you wanted.* Then she says, 'Hm. I am sure she will help, Mum. He is her brother. And she is just next door.' She will make an accusation of that too.

'Anyway,' says her mother in a response that's not a response and which therefore tells Meli exactly what she is thinking, 'how are my little darlings?' Changing the subject, pointedly, she thinks this suggests that she is being gracious. But if you have to *think* yourself gracious, chances of you conveying this are slim. What you are in fact doing is an act of passive aggression. It's a dismissal of a conversation where you don't agree with the other's point of view. She is hurt because she feels abandoned by Meli, but she could never say it. Instead she implies it because if you only imply something it can always be denied as misunderstanding. It's a child's play.

'Good, they are good.' Meli says slightly bristled at the "little darlings". She doesn't care about the dismissal. She knows shortly her mother will go onto talk about her brother's children. The question about Meli's two are a mere precursor for this compare game that she cannot resist. In her daughter-in-law, Meli's mum found a new object to project all the misgivings she has ever had about her own self.

'Ah, that's good. Bennie's kids are ill again. They have been to school one out of seven weeks this term, sadly. But what can you do when no one listens to me. She should have taken them to a specialist two years ago. None of this would be happening. If I told them once.' Every word loaded with tacit disapproval. It was depressing to Meli, the predictability of this accusation, this disapproval directed at the woman parent, not the man parent. Women do things to women. Why can't they see that?

When Meli says, 'Well, kids get ill, you know, I am sure they will grow out of it...'

Her mother interrupts, triumphantly, 'Not yours! My little

darlings, they are something else, aren't they?' There is an affection in her mother's voice when she speaks about Eliza and Burt that makes Meli shudder. It feels so dissonant, her words, her tone, softness that is unfamiliar, unlike Meli's experience of her mother.

Meli makes herself ignore this feeling and return to defend the other woman in this conversation. 'They are quite busy, aren't they. She works long days,' she says, trying once again to reposition her mother in relation to the world where not everything is a question of good or bad.

'Yes, I suppose they are, but, Meli,' - her mother implores, one more try to get Meli to go along with her disapproval, - 'so are you and you are doing it mostly alone. And,' still not finished, 'when I was there the last time she hadn't sorted the kids' clothes in two weeks. The drawers are all untidy and you can't find things you are looking for and when you do the clothes are three sizes too small.' Condemnation overload.

Meli doesn't want to store it for her mother. And so she only says 'Hm.'

Then her mother says, 'I was surprised that your brother will be coming over but he is coming to help.' She is talking about Meli's brother offering to come over to help around while father is bedridden. It is not surprising to Meli at all that her brother would do that. He is a nice guy. She knows it isn't surprising to her mother either, but by saying that, she is also saying that he is coming and Meli isn't. There is more than one way to make a cat feel guilt. Or, perhaps her mother doesn't mean it like that. Perhaps it's all in Meli's head. But if it is, where did it come from?

They finish the conversation shortly after this. As Meli disconnects the call she feels sad, bad and she feels mad. She feels sad for her mother who can't rid herself of the bad feelings someone else had put in her in their time, and she feels mad at her mother for making Meli feel bad about feeling mad, and she feels mad at herself for letting it get to her. Her mother has a rigid mindset that says some things won't change, I won't change, *I* am not capable of change. This is the thing that infuriates Meli because she knows that everything is open to change. If only she tried. But she won't. Instead she keeps projecting all the feelings she can't bear into the world, expecting it to hold it for her like an infant does when it cries of hunger or discomfort or fear, incapable of taking up an agency to help itself, incapable of thinking for itself. Meli's mother is a staunch believer in things being just one of those things and that being what it was because then you don't need to think for yourself.

Or are mothers but scarecrows, crude diagrams, denied existence of their own. Are they creatures we make up to define ourselves against? Are they Voodoo dolls for our own desires, hate, our deficiencies?

Who said this? Not Meli.

Chapter 17

Tor is in Prison

1980s-1990s

A small town in a little country

Meli walks down to the matron's office. She wants to break into a run but she stops herself. She knows her life is not going to be the same once she picks up that telephone receiver. That is a fact. The only question is, by how much?

'Hello?' A neutral tone to welcome the change that's coming, apprehensive but not scared.

'Meli, it's Cynthia, Tor's mum.'

She never thinks of Tor's mum by her name. It all sounds surreal already. Tor is Meli's Serious Boyfriend.

Meli and Tor first met at a nightclub. Tor was seeing someone else at the time so all they did was have a conversation and make a mental note. Then, about two weeks later, they bumped into each other in town, and Meli smiled at him. Tor later said that smile was the deal breaker. He was in love. He left his girlfriend and started walking in places he thought he might bump into Meli. It was the time before mobile phones.

Tor likes reading books about Mafia. So does Meli. But she never thinks of them as prescriptive. In fact, she doesn't think of most things as prescriptive, including recipes. Tor is also very smart and is in the third year of a good university, studying economics. His dad is a lawyer and he is rumoured to have worked for the KGB. No one in town likes him, but everyone is scared of him so everyone's children who are now almost adults want to be Tor's friend. His mother is a matron at another secondary school, in their hometown. She is nice. But she never calls Meli.

'Meli, I have something I need to tell you.'

Silence. Meli is thinking, people waste so much time by saying things which are obvious and unnecessary to say. It is always a preparation for something but all it does is increase anxiety because you know whatever it is, it's not going to be good and now you have to wait two sentences longer.

'Tor is in Austria and he won't be coming back for six months.'

'In Austria? Like Vienna Austria?'

This is at least weird, possibly worrying, but doesn't sound like anyone died, which is good. Tor was meant to be coming to pick her up this Friday. They were planning on going to his parents' holiday home for a treat. He said he had something to tell her.

'Yes.'

'Did you say six months?' She might have misheard. Maybe she said six days.

'Yes. He did something silly and he is...' Cynthia hesitates for a second, clears her throat and then forces it out, 'on remand.' She lowers her voice as if someone might overhear her in her empty flat from where she is calling. Meli barely hears her. There is really no need to whisper. 'He has been remanded in custody pending a court hearing,' she adds when Meli doesn't say anything.

'I see.' Meli says finally, not seeing at all. She holds onto the telephone receiver so hard it might embed itself there. She is sweating suddenly, and her heart is in her mouth. She can't speak. She doesn't know what to say to this woman called Cynthia who is her boyfriend's mum, so she waits.

'What I was wondering was, would you like to come and visit him?' Cynthia goes on gently like you might if you trod on something and you are willing it to not be crushed under your weight. 'We are going to go this weekend. I know it is difficult with the exams next week but I thought you might want to…'

'Yes,' Meli interrupts her, 'I will come.'

'Ok.'

'Meli?'

'Yes?'

'It will be ok,' Cynthia says more to herself than Meli.

In the end it wouldn't be ok, of course. That kind of happy ending has no place in Meli's life story.

But in the beginning, on his return, it will look like it could be. Tor will come out of prison, his long hair cut short, no more Mr Nice Guy, just a nice guy from now on. He will bring Meli eighteen red roses. He has missed her birthday and they will make love and they will make dreams about their future. But even as their bodies remember their old ways in the lost and found search for each other, she feels it, the disconnect. Their future will not see them together. She will be desperately sad about this for a long time. She loves him. He is the first person she chooses in her life with whom she begins the process of self-actualisation. Why did he have to ruin it?

Despite all the embracing being with Tor just isn't the same, try as they might. She feels so disconnected from him that she cannot remember how to be with him. He is becoming a stranger in her bed. She starts going out without him, and things happen. It feels to her their relationship now is like a thing that someone cut in half and was then expecting it to grow back together just by willing it. *Go on, you can do it, you did it before, you can feel like that again.* But she can't. Meli's love is not yet capable of holding together things which come apart. Meli can't regenerate the lost connection. She cannot wait. She hadn't waited for Tor. Not really. He was not there. She could not hold onto him in her mind. He became elusive like something that wasn't real. She just could not do it. Life is too short to wait for your first serious boyfriend for too long. People who take things seriously might do that, maybe because people who take things seriously are shown how to hold onto a good thing. Maybe that's why they are serious. Meli is not interested in becoming a serious person.

Back in the room she asks, 'Gabi, what do you wear when you go to visit your boyfriend in a prison?'

Gabi says, 'Shiii-it, Mels, how is your life so full of shit?'

Chapter 18

Leaving Things Behind

2020

A small town in a little country

Meli is at her aunt's house. She smokes a cigarette, black coffee ominous in the cup, brewing up a storm as she stirs in the sugar. Her make up is smudged around her eyes. She was crying earlier, but she is done with that.

'I am leaving,' Meli says to her aunt.

'You are over-reacting, Meli,' her aunt says with no conviction. She sounds a bit scared, actually.

'No. It is not just about today. I refuse to live like this. It's just not an option.'

Her mother screamed at her earlier that day. She said, the least she could do was pay rent, even though she wasn't yet earning any money. Meli wondered what it meant, *the least she could do*. The least she could do for being such a horrible person? The least she could do was to pay her mother for providing some threadbare needs like a roof over her child's head and a bed to sleep in? Because she gives her exactly fuck all else according to Meli's quick calculation.

Mother was angry about something Meli said or didn't say, and not quite knowing what to do, and her emotional repertoire being what it was, she asked her daughter for money. It was to show her who was in charge when all was said and done. Except her mother isn't the sort of a person who is in charge. Meli felt deeply resentful. She felt like she was the one who looked after her mother for as long as she could remember. At first, it made them close. Little girls like playing as grown-ups. Another thing about little girls is that they take sides when they see one giant, which is how adults appear to a small child, shouting at another smaller giant. They don't see that shouting can sometimes be a cover up for crying. When a big giant hits the smaller giant, it gets scary, but little girls are intuitive and the drive to survive is powerful. They sometimes find a way, but not without a cost. So, at first Meli didn't mind looking after her mother. Later, that came later. When it came, it hit hard. It made Meli resent her mother for not letting her have a childhood. They went from too close to too far apart Never the right distance, that is the problem. They can't get the distance right.

Someone probably told her mother to do that, to demand that Meli pay rent. Meli is outraged. What makes it even more infuriating is that her mother regretted it almost as soon as she said it. Typical, thinks Meli. At the age of eighteen, most things in the world are divided into either proving or disproving Meli's point, usually proving. Meli does not see her mother as a woman who needs help herself from another adult. What she sees is an incompetent adult who can never see things through, who can't own her actions, her decisions. It is always someone else that makes her do it.

In relation to their relationship, everything is Meli's fault.

It's even Meli's fault her mother could not mother her in a way which would not make Meli feel like everything is always her fault. Meli is a fault of her own.

It's like when you are bumped by a person pushing a trolley and it really hurts you and the person apologises and when you don't readily accept their apology, with a smile or whatever, everyone who sees the incident starts feeling sorry for the person who pushed the trolley into you because you didn't say *don't worry, it's ok*. But it isn't fucking ok. It hurts. The people watching, they end up getting mad at you, *come on, she didn't mean it, for God's sake, would you look at her, who does she think she is?* You can hear them muttering not very quietly. You end up the one in the wrong. *She apologised, didn't she, what else can she do?* Just like that, the victim of the trolley bumping is the bad guy. No one remembers she was the one who got hurt. Life sucks as far as Meli can tell. The only thing she can think of is to get as far away from it as she can. Getting away from things that hurt will be her thing, working the distance.

She promises herself again, while telling her mother also, she will never be like her, weak and inconsistent. Her mother will always utilise other people to try to make Meli feel guilty. Meli has wondered more than once what the fuck is she supposed to do with all this guilt. If only you could sell guilt. *Just look how she treats me*, she would say to a nonplussed visiting relative, *Look how she speaks to me*, to a shopping assistant in their local veg store. It's so pathetic, so infuriating. She just can't meet Meli, mind to mind or heart to heart. Their connection is like a malfunctioning radio-frequency identification, waves in a futile search of a frequency, just a horrible creaking noise. That is the sum of their relationship.

When Meli finally speaks she says she doesn't think so, there is really nothing to pay for here, and then she packs her things.

'I am never coming back,' she says to her mother as she puts her shoes on. Her mother is a sore sight, hovering there, hands covering her face, just not finding the words.

'Meli. What are you doing?'

'I'm not coming back home. I don't even want to call it that, Home is a nice word. There is nothing nice about here.'

And with that knife twisted in, she leaves.

The tears come as soon as she is out of her mother's sight. This hurts more than she has expected.

'What are you leaving, Meli, what are you really leaving,' asks her aunt, 'because I'm thinking, it will go with you.'

'No. I am leaving *here*, this stupid little town with its stupid little people. I don't want to end up like them.'

'Like me,' her aunt says.

'It's different,' she says, feeling guilty, but thinking, well, yes, you too.

'Meli, what happened with Tor?'

'Nothing much. We broke up.'

'Why?'

'Someone told him some lies.'

'I see.'

Why did people have to do that? Say, *I see*. It's dishonest. Why not just say *I don't believe you but we don't have to talk about it*.

'Yes. Anyway, it's all done, that.'

'Where are you going to go?'

'I don't know. I think I might go to Germany.'

'Germany,' her aunt definitely sounds scared now. 'What are you going to do in Germany?'

'Not sex for money, don't worry, Aunty. I will only do sex for fun. For money, I will do some waitressing to start with. I'm

95

going with Johnny. He goes there for work and knows people. It will be good to earn some money and see a bit of the world.'

'I don't think that's a good idea. You told grandma?'

'Not yet'.

Aunty didn't ask if Meli told her mother. Anyway, she will soon find out. No chance for secrets to fester in this hellhole.

Chapter 19

Johnny

2020

A small town in a little country

'Who is Johnny?' Her aunt asks.

'He is a guy,' Meli says, 'a guy, I met. He is nice.'

This is the end of that conversation. Meli leaves her aunt's house shortly after and she won't see her again for the next fifteen years.

Johnny is indeed one of life's nice guys and he will look after Meli if she goes with him. Meli is thinking it will be a bit like going abroad fruit-picking minus the fruit. Johnny is good to look at, which is important because people who are good to look at usually make friends more easily and Meli could do with making new friends. Also, Johnny knows people and because people like him, and he likes people, Johnny is quite a good person to be around when you don't like yourself very much at all. Finally, Johnny is responsible. She only needs this for a bit, this steadying influence of a good person, to soak it in, to find her feet again, because she lost her feet, or some part of herself anyway, with Tor finding out things she didn't want to hurt him with.

She met Johnny in a bar, when Tor was away, and Johnny became a friend. Johnny hoped to be much more than that and Meli had wrongly given him ideas that made Johnny hope he wasn't hoping in vain. Or rather, Meli had given him ideas that made Johnny wrongly hope. She didn't mean to be unkind. She thought that he would understand that you cannot start a new relationship when your boyfriend is in prison. You can definitely do other things though because life is too short. But that was a different thing and Johnny didn't understand this. It seemed to Meli, men never understood women like women understood other women. It would have been clear to every girl in the dorm that Johnny never would be more than a friend whom she occasionally let have his way with her. Some would disapprove, sure, but they would still understand. That is the thing about women. Anyway, Johnny is nice. He makes Meli feel nice from time to time. But she can't feel nice for too long. Meli feels a little bit sad for him but that isn't going to stop her.

After two months in Berlin, Meli leaves Johnny in Germany one night. She gives him no warning. He cries. He begs her to stay. He is worried about her. Where will she go? What will she do? She hardly has any money. She can't just walk out into the world like that. Alone. A woman. He is so responsible. And he is so wrong. She isn't responsible or right. What she is, is angry and anger can take you far.

Another two months of her life in a paragraph. She is so excited about the next one. It's like a book you never want to end.

Chapter 20

Classical History of a Life With a Newborn

1990s-2000s

Central London

This is necessarily a story about women, because men can't have babies, writes Meli, in the margins of her frustratingly long-taking draft introduction to her MA dissertation in Classical History. *Topic: Females in Classical Athens; Seclusion or Self-Isolation, Fact and Fiction.* Her hypothesis is that women were not secluded against their will. And, if it wasn't against their will, whatever it was, it was not seclusion. It is true, Meli writes, they didn't become a Pericles, they couldn't vote and they did most of the household management. But, everything in the world starts with good household management. Nothing good can ever come from a badly run home in whichever way, and nothing can ever come to be without a woman because men can't have babies.

I will assess the impact of woman's competence in her role as the household manager to explore whether it is appropriate to equate the female position in classical Athenian society with bodily or emotional

99

constraint, political ineptitude and derision and disrespect, as interpreted by some scholars, leading to the generally accepted, yet highly questionable, opinion of women of this period. Too long, Meli. The sentence is way too long. I will come back to that later, another note in the margin.

The key concern for the citizens was their home. And, if something is the key, then you need it to open the treasure box and nothing else will do unless you want to start breaking things down.

I will argue that in such circumstances, women were in fact fully autonomous despite the seeming preservation of social appearances where men appear to be ascribed more "important" roles, usually ones in the public domain. I will argue that women's responsibilities became theirs naturally, given physiological facts such as menstruation, pregnancy, childbirth and lactation and so on.

And, physical strength, too, thinks Meli. You might not actually feel like ploughing the fields if you can instead sit down, have a cup of coffee and make clothes for yourself and your family while catching up on recent developments with your friends. Lysistrata showed the world of Athens and beyond quite clearly the power the women held, didn't it? Meli brushes aside the annoying voice in her head that says, yes, a story of women invented by a man who invested all their power in their sex. Brush, brush, brush. Paint over. Women commonly ran the household accounts. They knew how much flour there was in the house and they knew all that happened in the Parliament because the men would come home and tell their wives all about it, needing an opinion. They were a team, Meli will argue, a team who agreed on their respective responsibilities, by and large, because they made sense at the time. Things would go on to change, of course, but that didn't mean women were second-class citizens in any way, did it?

Does your anatomy determine your autonomy? It must

shape it at least. And this can't be a question of fair or not because for once, Meli will say it, biology is what it is. It is a science. Mostly, if you are a woman, although you may not have children because you can't, or because you decide not to. As a man, you will never have this choice or this ordeal. And that must be a matter of great regret to men. They might even envy you and so they will have to make you believe you need them, as a woman, which you might have once, in the absence of a tractor, say, which would have made you a team. The all-knowing human-life-giving woman was happy to go along with appearances which made her man feel more manly. Women would do this not because they were subservient, they did this, and continue to do this, as they are more compassionate than men. It is because they bear the pain of giving life. No woman has ever willingly started a war. But many women have died starting a life for someone else.

Meli gathers evidence to make her case. It isn't hard. Like with everything, if you go looking for someone to agree with you, you will always find them. If Meli set out to do a dissertation arguing that women in classical Athens *were* secluded and isolated, she would find it easily. She knows this but she disregards this, dismisses it like an annoying fruit fly. It's just a matter of interpretation. There were plenty of recorded court speeches from the period and there was Aristotle and his comedy, which was actually not comedy at all, but more a social anthropology, and it was all there easy to see, and not that funny either. You just need to make a compelling argument of it.

Lawyers like gathering evidence and Meli isn't enough of a free thinker yet to see the problem with her argument, which is that it is not free. It is predicated upon something inside Meli that she hasn't yet met. At this point, Meli will fight her point by factual opposition, but it lacks nuance and it lacks the wholeness of truth. It's just a contour because there is nothing easy or quick about arriving anywhere close to any truth. And internalised misogyny is like an octopus, too many tentacles and all under the cover of the deep, dark sea of our unconscious mind.

Burt is crying. He is five months now. He is the most incredible event of Meli's life so far. He turns her to jelly. She sings songs to him. She sings when he is having a bath, when she is pushing him in his pram in the Bunhill Fields, when she feeds him. She sings and she is surprised to discover she has a singing voice. She never used to sing much. Not as a child, because to sing you actually have to feel like singing.

'Meli?'

Don can't find his glasses. She knows exactly where they are. She is not singing anymore.

'They are where you left them,' she shouts from downstairs, carefully extricating Burt from his swaddling blanket.

'That's not helpful,' Don bats back.

'I know. It is irritating. As is the fact you keep ignoring good advice. Like always put them in the same place and you will never have this fucking problem, which you then make into *my* problem,' she says, walking upstairs, Burt in her arms, crying. 'I think he is hungry.'

Breastfeeding is not going smoothly. It is either too much or not enough, or, more like it is too much and therefore not enough. Burt is a hungry baby and he goes at it like a wolf and then when it hits his little oesophagus too hard, it promptly returns back up, burning on its way up. She has started using bottles a couple of times a day. It is making things much happier. She abandons nature and goes to the kitchen to warm up a bottle and the crying stops.

'They're under the newspapers in the office,' she says.

'You could have just said that.'

'You could have just put them in the bowl I got you specifically for that reason.'

'I don't not do it deliberately to piss you off, Meli.'

'I know you don't. But you also don't deliberately make it not happen, which is kind of the same thing. It is not a big deal to you. And you don't care to remember it is a big thing to me.'

'Why is it a big thing to you?'

'Because I hate that you use me like this – to remember for you, like you are too important to remember little shitty things like where you keep your fucking clothes, or where the frying pan is. Where is this? Where is that? All the fucking time. Like my purpose in life is to remember stupid, mundane, everyday shit while you are doing all the interesting stuff.'

'Ah, fucking hell, Mels. Life's too short. You're tired. Try and grab a nap when Burt does,' says Don The Normaliser, as he grabs his glasses and runs out of the door, kissing Meli briefly on her cheek. He is running late. He is going to an important meeting.

Looking at the vomit on her arm, her breast hanging out of her top like an alien, Burt crying again with his reflux and the pile of unwashed laundry on the bathroom floor, Meli's dissertation suddenly feels like a big bad farce.

Chapter 21

Humans and Wolves

1990S-2000S

Central London

They come out of the maternity wing of the city hospital. The sun is high and it greets them at the door like a magnificent host, with open arms, welcome, come on in. Meli is with Don, who is pushing the pram, her arm in his and the other one resting on her stomach. Her stomach is filled with baby goodness. Don has taken time from his important work to come with her to her important meeting. And the meeting went well, glorious black and white and grey of the ultrasound colours, the beat of the heart, the cold gel on her skin.

'Unbelievable. She is a genius already,' Meli says, grin on her face.

Don smiles. He likes to see Meli do that one-sided grin thing. It means things are at least half right.

Their baby-girl, who is all of five months in utero, has turned. This is not usually a matter of celebration but in this instance it is. Meli was not going to be delivering another child "naturally". Only men who never gave birth, and women who have identified with this ridiculous, cruel point of view, could give this process such a name. She will challenge any man to imagine their pelvis having to move out of their *natural* place to allow a small human head to emerge from within and to call that natural. That is not to mention flesh tearing and hard Victorian metal objects being used sometimes to help extract the said head. And, as Meli read in a helpful article recently, in very rare cases, "the laxity leads to the separation of the pubic bones either before or after delivery which makes walking very difficult". So, yeah, it was about as natural as using your hands for walking. Just because some can do it, doesn't make it natural.

'Natural. I swear if they use that word again...'

'Well, animals do it, I guess,' Don says, interrupting but non-committal, 'so, I suppose in some way, you could say it is natural.'

'Animals also kill each other for status. Or, to sort out their differences. Or, just because they feel threatened. Is that something we aspire to hold on to?'

'True,' says Don, 'and also for a shag. Which seems a bit more fun. Status brings responsibility for your herd, or whatever group of animals we are imagining.'

'I'm thinking gorillas, and I'm thinking all those things are mainly fought for by male animals,' says Meli, 'and, once you have status, I suspect you get all the shag you want. Probably more than you want.'

'Wolves don't,' Don says.

'They don't what?'

'I think it is a female wolf that leads a wolf pack. Or, at least they are on the same par with males. It's about the strongest and the wisest. There's no sexual discrimination. And elephants, they are matriarchs with a capital M.' Don smiles, pleased with his little joke he didn't know was coming.

'That's encouraging. Did you know, according to a study I read recently, every day this year, almost 800 women died from preventable causes related to pregnancy and childbirth. A maternal death occurred almost every two minutes last year. More than 300,000 women die from pregnancy every year.' She fires these off like bullets into an invisible target because it is invisible, but it is there.

Don is silent.

Meli is not smiling anymore.

He gives her arm a squeeze and says, 'it will be ok, Meli-Wolf.'

She nods. The grin resurfaces as she feels a kick under her hand.

'I know. She knows what she needs to do. She is a feminist already.'

It will take exactly seven minutes for Eliza to come to this world. Nice, clean cut, meticulously working local anaesthesia administered in the calmness of an organised C-section procedure. There's a tiny bit of a burning flesh smell, and then the sweet squealing of a little baby wolf. No pain. There will be no pain at all when Eliza enters Meli's life story.

Chapter 22

The Little Read Riding Hood

1970s-1980s

A small town in a little country

And the end of all our exploring
Will be to arrive where we started
And know the place for the first time.
Through the unknown, remembered gate
When the last of earth left to discover
Is that which was the beginning;

T.S.Eliot

Meli is lying on her grandparents' bed. She is having a sleepover. She is not sure why she is but that doesn't matter. Being with her grandma is good. It is porridge with a bit of butter melted on top and sugar and coco. It is stories and it is having your head stroked, and a strand of hair put behind your ear, which tickles just the nicest bit. Her head rests in Grandma's lap, Grandma's hand gentle on Meli's head. It feels warm and soft and Meli is pretending in her head that she lives here with her grandma. A black and white wedding picture hangs above the bed. Grandma looks like a princess. Grandad is a handsome, young man and so proud. They look happy. There is a strange gap between how they look in the picture and how they live. This sometimes makes Meli a bit sad but she doesn't quite know why.

Her grandma is reading her a story. It is Little Red Riding Hood. Meli is a bit old for it now but grandma doesn't have many books so they reread them or she makes them up. This one is not a jolly version in which the wolf runs off and is never to be seen again. It is the one where his stomach is cut open by the woodcutter to rescue the swallowed grandma and then its stomach is filled with heavy stones instead before he gets thrown down the deep well.

Grandad is next door, playing chess with his friend. These occasions are of great solemnity. The game will go on for hours. There will be a bottle of vodka, of course, to go with it. But it will be ok. The chess time is a calm time, vodka or not.

Meli is feeling a bit sorry for the wolf. Little Red Riding Hood didn't listen to her mum and strayed from the path. She knew there might be a wolf there. It's almost like she wanted to meet the wolf. Meli wonders if she would want to meet a wolf and what she would do if she did. She would definitely not fall for the silly cover up.

'Grandma?'

'Yes, my Meshi.'

'Why does the wolf have to eat little girls when there is plenty of food in the woods easier to catch without having to pretend he is a human grandma?'

'Hm. Maybe being a wolf, he can't help himself.'

Meli is not convinced. 'But, grandma.'

'Yes, Meshi.'

'It looks like the little girl can't help herself either? So why then does the wolf get punished? Little Red Riding Hood did something her mama said not to do. The wolf just did what wolves do. He ate food.'

'Meshi you are too clever for me. Maybe the story is a warning to little girls about listening to their mamas because there are dangerous things out there that they should avoid.'

'But, Grandma.'

'Yes, Meshi.'

'The wolf eats Grandma. And she is not a little girl and she didn't do anything wrong and she didn't even go out.'

'Ah, that is true, Meshi, but, when you get old, like grandmas do, you don't always think clearly. Your brain gets a little muddled up. You might think it is your lovely granddaughter at the door and yet it is someone else who means you harm.'

Meli is silent for a while. 'Grandma, I think this story is all wrong. The wolf can't think to stop itself from being mean, but it can pretend being a human grandma, which I think means he can think, just not in a good way. The girl doesn't listen to her mama but she is not told off at all, and Grandma is too old to think clearly. This is not a good story, Grandma. It makes no sense. It just makes you feel scared but it doesn't make sense. I don't like it when things don't make sense. And I don't like to feel scared. I think it would be better if the wolf and the girl could talk it out, when they bump into each other. They could make sense of things and then no one needs to be scared. Maybe they could even be friends. And Grandma needs someone to remind her to not open her doors to strangers.'

'Meshi, I think that is a different story.'

Meli is thinking. There is something else about this story that is giving her butterflies. She would also stray from the path if she was the girl because it seemed exciting. But she won't tell Grandma this. Meli is not sure why. She doesn't really keep secrets from Grandma. She will think about this tomorrow. It would probably worry her, Meli tells herself, but she knows somehow that is not all of it.

'Grandma? Why does your tummy make so much noise?' She grins, enjoying her joke.

'It is probably thinking, Meshi.' But it is more like Grandma is thinking, she completely misses Meli's joke.

'What is it thinking about Grandma?'

'About the day we have had. It is digesting all the things we have said and done and thought, so we can have good dreams. It will keep the good bits in and get the bad ones ready to throw down the well.'

'Grandma, I think you are getting mixed up. You are mixing the story with real life,' Meli says, smiling, confused but intrigued.

'That is what happens, Meshi. We mix stories with real life. Life is like a soup, where the real bits and the story bits get all cooked up together and in the end you don't even know which ingredients you have put in anymore and which were there in the first place. And sometimes, even other people can throw their stories into your soup.'

'What, even when you grow up?'

'Yes. Especially when you grow up.'

Meli is thinking.

'But that must be confusing if you don't know what is real and what is a story and who put it in.'

'Yes. And that's why you have to take time to digest your food, Meshi.'

'You are not really talking about food, Grandma, are you?'

'No. But stories can be like food. Things that happen in life, can too. They feed you in some way. There is good food and there is bad food. And that's why when you go to bed, you ask yourself, when I was mean to that boy at school who is always a bit dirty, was it me, or was it the wolf from the story who was just being a wolf and wasn't thinking about other people's feelings?'

'You mean I put a bit of the story into my soup to see what it would taste like? I was trying on his skin like the wolf does when he swallows Grandma and pretends to be her?'

'Exactly, Meshi. You've got it. Sometimes we pretend to be someone we are not because it might get us something we want.'

Meli is thinking about the Little Red straying from the path.

'I know that already, Grandma, but I wasn't trying to get anything I wanted when I was mean to Milos.'

'No, Meshi. Why were you mean then?' Grandma is getting tired but there is something on Meli's mind that she wants to get out. She wants to frame it in a question.

'Do you think we sometimes want to pretend to be someone we are not just to try out what it would feel like to be someone else?'

'It is getting late, Meshi...'

'Or is it that we are all those things a little bit?' Meli finally finishes her thought.

'I don't know, Meshi. Shall we sleep on it?'

'Sure. One more thing, Grandma.'

'Ok. Meshi, one more thing.'

'I think my favourite story is the one with the Little Bunny Ears. It's babyish but I like it. I think I would like to go on an adventure like him, to see the world. And then I will come back and tell you all about it.'

'That sounds wonderful, Meshi. But you need to read more stories first. To see if that is the one you want to make your soup with.'

'Do we only have one story to make the soup with,

Grandma?'

'That depends, Meshi.'

'On what?'

'How much you get to read.'

'Oh. Well, I like reading, so I guess my soup could be really good.'

'Yes, Meshi, I really hope so.' Grandma sounds a little sad. She doesn't mean to but Meli can tell.

'Grandma?'

'Yes?'

'What is your favourite story?'

As if in answer, the empty bottle slams on the glass table top in the room next to them. 'Wilma,' Grandad's voice soaring through the thin walls, 'bring us another bottle, dear. And, a new pack of smokes.'

Grandma gets up immediately, tucking in Meli quickly planting a kiss on her head. Her Prince Charming does not like to be kept waiting, not anymore.

Meli is looking at the wedding picture, thinking about the gap between the story it tells and the real life. In the picture, Grandad looks like Prince Charming. Meli imagines he may have slayed seven-headed dragons to win Grandma over. And, Grandma, she looks like the girl who was made a princess. Except her life doesn't seem very princess-like. It is more like she is constantly covering up for Grandad's emperor's clothes so the people cannot see that he is not really any prince at all, just a shouting, ill-tempered man who didn't live up to his expectations of himself, in a nice Sunday suit.

Tomorrow, Meli thinks, I will ask Grandma if you can put a soup down the drain and cook a new one, or would that be a big waste and you had better just eat it. Like when you make your bed, you lie in it. Are second chances allowed? She will also ask another question about the wolf that is on her mind, the question she didn't ask today. The most obvious question to Meli is the one that made the least sense of all the other things that made no sense. Why didn't the wolf just eat the girl in the woods? Perhaps he did not want to eat her at all.

Chapter 23

A Sorry Hydra of Forgiveness

1990s-2000s

Central London

'What's that?' her mother asks.

'It is a monster with many heads, one of which is immortal.' Meli is doing a crossword.

'Strange name,' she says. Her mother is ironing something that doesn't need straightening.

'Yes, I guess, a bit over-specifying. It's from a Greek word for water,' Meli says absentmindedly. 'She was a serpentine monster. Her lair was the lake, which was an entrance to the underworld. She was killed by Heracles, so the story goes.'

'Oh,' says her mother.

'It was the second of the twelve jobs he had to do for King Eurystehus.'

'Why did he have to?'

'He killed his wife and two sons. It was a part of his atonement.'

'Oh my goodness, why did he do that?' asks Meli's mother.

'He doesn't sound very nice, I thought he was some kind of a hero.'

'He was, Mum. Sometimes, heroes don't start off as heroes, especially if they are illegitimate sons of gods. Hera made Heracles go momentarily mad because she hated him. Which was, you know, scapegoating,' adding, 'blaming the wrong guy.'

'Was it? Who was Hera and why did she hate what was his name again?'

Meli puts down the pencil and abandons the crossword. 'Hera was the goddess of marriage, women and family. Ironically, she was also the protector of women during childbirth. But she was jealous and vengeful as her husband, Zeus, the top guy on the Olympus, was a serial adulterer with many kids to his name and Heracles was a living reminder of one of her husband's infidelities.'

'Ah, I see now.' Mother says. 'That would make you quite cross.'

Meli says 'Yes, it would. Although, she could have just killed him, right? But that wasn't enough. She wanted him to suffer. There is no suffering in dying. So she induced this madness in him, which made him murder his wife and his two sons.'

'That's a sad story.' Meli's mother says.

'Yes, but it is also interesting, no? Who do you think was more powerful, Zeus or Hera?'

Her mother has been here for a few days now. They are sitting in the garden of their tiny flat. Don and Meli have recently bought it, their first home. It is small but it is theirs. She is looking at it from the garden, and it feels good looking at it. It feels good to say it. My flat. Their own home. They bought together.

Don is out on some work function and he is going to be

late. Today, Meli doesn't mind. Meli and her mother, they have some stuff they are talking about. Meli has been talking to her therapist about things and she has been getting ready to have a conversation with her mother. She feels a bit apprehensive but also quite excited about this. She has wanted to tell things to her mother for a long time now. They have been getting on for the past few years. It has become easier to be around each other with Don in the picture. It was as though he had taken over some territory and she no longer had a claim on it. Her mother renounced her right, which she felt was given to her when she gave birth to Meli, to expect symbiosis. When mothers give birth to daughters, a thing happens that does not happen when mothers give birth to sons. Mothers identify with their daughters. And if they are not careful, and they don't stop confusing what's theirs with what belongs to their daughters, some daughters will end up resenting their mothers. A lot. For a long time. Or they end up being their mothers, never knowing who they were supposed to be in their own right, in their own skin.

Right now, Meli and her mother are drinking wine and smoking cigarettes, sitting on wonky chairs to match their feelings, underneath an old cherry tree. They are listening to some old music. Meli's mother is crying.

'If I could do it all again,' she says, but she doesn't finish the sentence.

'It's ok, Mum.' Meli says, finally, but not too soon. 'It is ok now. I am sorry you are upset.' She says, but she just said a whole lot of things to upset her mother. *I am sorry you were not there when I needed you. I really am. I know you did your best. But it wasn't enough.*

'If I could do it again, if only I could do it again,' echoes the cave where the ghosts from the past have come to gather.

'We can't go back, Mum, but we do have now.'

'Yes,' her mother says, suddenly lighter, sensing hope like an animal who just perceived a way out, 'we do. And I will make it up to you, Meli. Please can you forgive me?' Her legs are crossed, her arms crossed, cigarette in her hand, tears and make up smudged. She is all crossed, like fingers might be to summon up hope. She looks pitiful and vulnerable.

Now Meli is crying. Her mother can't make it up to her. You can't undo something you have done. Your body keeps the score. This thing you have made, it can be a scar or it can be a lack. When something is done or not done when it should be, this thing cannot be undone. It lives in the past and the door is closed on that. The final curtain call is long gone, and the past lives on in you. Forever, it goes on living in you. What you can do, like a good renovator with a good apprenticeship, is keep going over it again and again, and with a bit of luck, it will one day feel solid enough and there will be a new thing. But underneath that thing, you know it, the scar or the lack will be there. And if you should one day feel wobbly, when too many things have been leaned against your new walls, well, it could collapse. It shouldn't be too hard to renovate the second time though, because there will be remaining structures to build on, and, because the body remembers how it's done. Muscle memory.

But that is not the point, not today. To be heard, to be really heard by her mother is to start to rewire those creaky old pathways, and that is probably the most important thing that can happen to a human being. They can change. They can change things that don't work. Meli finally feels heard by her mother. No excuses. No compensation either. Just that. It's an opportunity for something new to emerge. It has taken nearly thirty years. Weirdly, Meli remembers it was the same length of time that it took her country to decide to change its name and its identity. It split one thing to become two things, dropping a word in the process. After the initial euphoria, the country found creating a new identity is a process that does not end in one bloodless revolution. Also, how do you cut something in half without it bleeding?

They sit in silence now, the sun is setting down and the air gets cooler.

'Should we go in?'

'Yes, let's go and have some broth.'

Her mum does make the best chicken broth.

They eat in silence. It is a good silence. It is a silence cleared of any gravity. It hugs them comfortably and they put their feet up and watch something on TV that allows them both to revel in this new found moment. They are together but finally separate.

Later in bed, Meli is thinking about this evening. She is feeling lighter but she is not fooled. She knows lightness and heaviness are just two sides of the same coin. It depends on how you flip it.

She decides to message Don.

'Talked to Mum.'

Ping.

'And..?'

'And I think the act of forgiving is like killing Hydra.'

Ping.

'Err..?'

'It's a monster with nine heads, and not only is it a struggle to kill the first eight because they keep on growing back, but one of them can never be killed.'

Ping goes the phone again.

'Eight out of nine ain't bad honey.'

'Omg. Honey? Honey?? See you later. Or not.'

'I will be your Heracles.'

She doesn't reply.

'Or is it Hercules?'

Meli smiles. Don could always do that. He could always make her smile.

Going to sleep, Meli is thinks about stories of forgiveness and how it always seemed such a noble thing to do. But what the stories don't tell you is that forgiveness is a moving beast. It doesn't stay still. And it is a shape-shifter.

To be able to forgive at all, you have to really understand what it is you are forgiving despite all the shifts of shapes and explanations and excuses, in dance with time. Created like a true artist. It is because of these shape-shifts, which aim to conceal the truth, even from the artist himself, that the heads grow back. They grow back so you need to go there again and take a closer look. Look again, look them in the face that's fluid and delve deeper. See into the dark corner of the soul, and, even then, when you are finally done with all the chopping to bits, unpicking, even then, because of the lack or the scar, this thing that once happened or didn't, that last head cannot die. It stays there, resting if you are in peace, but it can recoil at you and snarl like an angry beast again. That is the best it gets. It is the best Meli can figure out so far. The best you can do is to keep the beast in check. Greet it with kindness and compassion when it comes up, like an old friend. Talk it down. Hold it tight, which you can because you understand how it all happened now, and someone you loved said sorry. And someone you loved, who died, lives on in you with her compassion and kindness to flood the world.

In this understanding lies the capacity for the new beginning, which is the true value of forgiving. It is when you put the pen down and say, I finally figured this one out. Now, I know the story I was given, but it isn't mine. Now, I can see how it was that I have strayed from my own path. It is because someone I trusted took me by my hand and walked me that way. They didn't mean to get me lost. It just happened. But I have retraced my steps, and now I can see sketches and contours of my own story on the horizon. It is greener, but it also needs colouring in. And I also know now to walk alone or with someone, if I choose. And that's how you rewrite the stars and become an author of your own story.

'I must write this down.' Meli says out loud to the room, and then she is asleep.

The following morning, there is a family of foxes sitting where Meli and her mother sat the day before. Mum, Dad and five baby foxes. One day it's you, and the next day it's foxes. We all have a turn, Meli is thinking, looking out of her kitchen window at this peaceful scene made up of wild animals in a London suburb.

We all have a turn to rewrite our beginning.

Chapter 24

Saying Goodbyes

2020s

London, outside of the M25

'What's funny about that?' Eliza asks, overhearing Don talking to the gardener outside her bedroom window. It was something about fertilising some trees.

'Nothing, I don't think,' says Meli.

'Why did Dad laugh then?'

'To be polite.'

'Ugh. That seems dumb.'

'It's not dumb, it's being considerate of someone else's feelings, Eliza.'

'Is it like when you said to your visitors recently that you are forever falling asleep with me when you take me to bed?' She puts air quotation marks around forever as she says this, which somehow makes the remark more cutting than enquiring despite the questioning intonation. Eliza is growing up and some things about growing up are not so nice, like when you experiment with being original but you end up being catty.

'You said that to be polite didn't you, because you didn't feel like going back in there. You didn't want to say, "hey guys, I am bored now." So basically, you lied.'

'I wasn't bored. I was tired. I didn't lie.'

'Then why did you go to read in your bed after you took me to bed?'

'Because I like reading before I go to sleep, Eliza.'

'Half-truth, Ma, half-truth.' And she gives Meli a look that makes them both smile.

'I love you, Horrid Henry.' Meli pulls Eliza in and covers her head in kisses.

'Eeew. Is this all I am good for, Mother?'

'This is what you are the best for, Daughter.' Meli whispers, as she leaves her nose pressed against her daughter's cheek, breathing her in, silent for a few seconds. These precious seconds which feel more revitalising than an hour deep tissue massage. Eliza gently breaks the embrace and scrutinises her mother's face, sensing the shift in Meli's composure.

They are in Meli's room. Opposite her bed is an alcove, some structural irregularity of the old house, now a shrine to memories that will never die, sheltering her most precious selection of pictures. Meli stares over Eliza's head at her grandma's face. She met Eliza when she was a few months old. That is the picture next to the wedding, the black and white one. The third picture is one of Meli, her mother and her grandma. That one feels the most complicated, three women sitting next to each other, sombre, close and foreboding. Grandma is wearing a beautiful night dress and a dark blue velvet dressing gown. She looks like she is breaking. She was breaking.

It was October two years ago. Meli was back home a few

months before Grandma was due to be moved to a nursing home. During the visit, they went walking in the old town cemetery to put some flowers on Granddad's grave and Meli took Grandma to have her hair done. Her black hair by now a shining soft silver, still so beautiful. She needed a walking stick these days and on their way home she hailed a taxi. It was so unlike her. This admission of her own frailty, this sudden surrender to her age blindsided Meli, knocking her heart to the bottom of her stomach. Grandma didn't tell Meli how bad things had got. She didn't want Meli to know she was in pain the whole time. This was the last story Grandma was telling her. Cancer was eating her alive, an angry parasite feasting on her ailing body until there would be nothing left.

Earlier in the day, Meli's mother bathed Grandma and her sore. When Meli saw it, she froze and then she puked. It was the most hideous thing Meli would ever see in her life. The wound so grotesque, so big and incongruous on her tiny grandma's beautiful body, a body that Meli used to rest her head on, listening to the heartbeat that would calm the worst storms in Meli's head.

Meli loved her mother then for being able to stand it, for not making Grandma feel like she was too hideous to touch. She made the sore clean and made Grandma smell nice again. She saw something in her mother that day that she has never seen before, some capability to put her feelings aside for someone else's feelings to be contained in this act.

They went over to Grandma's home after dinner.

They sat down, the three of them, in Grandma's living room. That was where they took that photo, in the room with a yellow, flowery wallpaper, the room that has seen many chess matches and many bottles of vodka come and go. That was a long time ago though. Granddad was dead nearly twenty years now. Only his rocking chair carrying on with the pretence of life that was long gone, creaking if someone banged into it. No one would ever sit in it and no one would ever walk in his shoes again.

Grandma looked so small this October night, but her hands were the same soft as Meli always remembered, they were sitting together, remembering things. Do you remember when is a sentence starter to something that will make you laugh or cry, or both. It is always something to remember.

'Do you remember when we played badminton on the dirt-road on those summer holidays, late into the night?' Grandma was tanned and beautiful and young. The summer breeze, warm and gentle, smoothing their burned skin.

'Do you remember those trips to the hairdresser?' Grandma would have her hair permed into position and Meli would get a mouthful of hairspray as she squeaked with excitement 'Can I have some, please, Grandma.'

'The smell of the chicken soup in your old kitchen?'

And so it went on.

Meli thought about the smell of Grandma's skin when she kissed her, cupping her cheeks in her soft hands. The lavender scent of her hand cream she never changed.

The dress ups in Grandma's clothes.

She remembered holding her breath watching Grandma put on her lipstick, shaped by the contour of her smile. She always looked so neat and quietly proud. Always thoughtfully done up but never too much. You need the right amount so no one can guess the shame and the pain hidden behind the dignified elegance.

The stories read and the stories made up.

The baking when Grandma would let her do it and make mess and she didn't care one bit.

The making of Meli's favourite sweets – suhajdy.

The day when Meli learned to swim. The warmth of grandma's smile, 'you did it, Meshi. You did it.' Those words, again and again.

The day when Meli broke the sink in Grandma's shop as she was swinging on it while Grandma was quietly arguing with Meli's mum.

The day when Meli introduced Don.

Grandma said, 'He is a good man, Meli, make sure you keep him happy.'

'I love you so much, *Starka*.' Meli was crying. It was too much. She wanted to hold on to those memories and never let them go. Never let her go.

'I love you too, my Meshi. Look at you, a beautiful woman, so many qualifications I can't even remember them, beautiful husband and children. You did it all, Meshi. What a soup. I am so proud of you.' And then she whispered, 'Do you remember *My Little Bunny Ear?*'

They held hands, crying together. They were holding something between them, you couldn't see it, you could only feel it, and it felt so heavy, neither of them wanting to let go of it. It was forty-three years of love.

Then her mother walked in, Meli's mother, Grandma's daughter, three generations of women, three stories. She had walked out earlier. She didn't want to cry. She didn't want to admit the sadness that was there. Didn't want to sit with it. She didn't want to see that Meli was saying goodbye to her mother. That was too much. She can handle a cancer sore, but not goodbyes. They all have different superpowers, the women in Meli's life.

She walked in and said loudly, defying the truth, 'That's enough, both of you, that's enough.' But to Meli, it wasn't enough, to Meli, her time with Grandma would never be enough. 'It's not, Mum. We still have a bit more time left,' she said.

The funeral was three months later. Grandma hated the idea of a nursing home. She didn't belong there. There was no one there to tell stories to. So she died. Meli was forty three years old that year. Meli's grandma was forty three years old when Meli was born. Meli knew Grandma waited until she would be ready. So she had to be, otherwise, she wouldn't have gone. But from that day, Meli would always be desperate for one more story.

'Mum. Mum.'

'Yes, darling.'

'Where are you? Because you are not here with me right now.'

'No. I was thinking about something.'

'I know,' says Eliza, 'you were thinking about Great-Grandma.'

'I don't want you to be sad, Mama.'

'You can only be sad if you have something to be sad about when you don't have it anymore, and that's a win, Eli.'

'Well, but you have something right here and you can kiss my head if you like?'

'I'd love that, Eli.'

'And remind me tomorrow, I must tell you a story I know.'

'What about?'

'A bunny with weird ears.'

'Ok, sure. Sounds funny.'

Meli holds her daughter tight and kisses her head and in no time at all Eli's breathing slows and deepens and she is asleep and her children in her arms, safe and at peace clothed in pyjama happiness, she knows it is easily the best thing she will ever have.

Acknowledgements

Firstly, thank you Lasavia, my publisher, for making this happen. Thank you to Rowan, my editor, for making me more friendly with speech marks and for all the gentle tidy up of my wordsy rainforest.

Thank you to the women in my life without whom this book also couldn't have happened. Gabi, for always standing by me, covering for me, laughing with me, worrying for me and never judging. Amy, for the belly laughs, oh my god, you could even make the school runs fun. For always being there and sometimes, for crying for me when I couldn't. For reading my book when it was only an infant crying for help, saying nice things which helped it grow. Hayley. For all the time you always find for me. For your immensely thoughtful words about everything and always. Rachel, Christina, Chantal and Susie. How lucky for me to have met you. Krish and Emma, thank you for being there at a different time of my life. The Before Children time when we were busy trying to be adults in our first jobs, but I still had a lot of growing up to do.

Finally, but it is a bottomless well, Danny. Thanks for bearing with me all these years. For your love and support. Without you, I wouldn't be me.